Marx Joyce
Abbott Machiavelli Chesterton Cooper Emerson
Hardy Montaigne Austen
Defoe Melville Haggard Hugo
Christie Eliot Grimm
Stoker Carroll Molière
Wilde Maupassant Byron
Engels Schiller
Garnett Einstein Fitzgerald Smith
Goethe Hawthorne Kafka
Cotton Dostoyevsky Hall
Baum Kipling Doyle Willis
Leslie Dumas Henry Nietzsche
Flaubert Turgenev Balzac
Stockton Vatsyayana Crane
Burroughs Whitman
Verne
Curtis Tocqueville Gogol Vinci
Homer Widger Tolstoy Busch
Darwin Thoreau
Potter Freud Twain Plato Scott
Zola Lawrence
Kant Jowett Stevenson Dickens
Andersen Cervantes Burton Hesse Harte
London Descartes
Poe Aristotle Wells Voltaire
Hale James Hastings
Cooke
Bunner Shakespeare
Richter Chekhov Chambers Irving
da
Doré Swift Dante Shaw Wodehouse Benedict Alcott
Pushkin
Newton

AF670397

tredition®

tredition was established in 2006 by Sandra Latusseck and Soenke Schulz. Based in Hamburg, Germany, tredition offers publishing solutions to authors and publishing houses, combined with worldwide distribution of printed and digital book content. tredition is uniquely positioned to enable authors and publishing houses to create books on their own terms and without conventional manufacturing risks.

For more information please visit: www.tredition.com

TREDITION CLASSICS

This book is part of the TREDITION CLASSICS series. The creators of this series are united by passion for literature and driven by the intention of making all public domain books available in printed format again - worldwide. Most TREDITION CLASSICS titles have been out of print and off the bookstore shelves for decades. At tredition we believe that a great book never goes out of style and that its value is eternal. Several mostly non-profit literature projects provide content to tredition. To support their good work, tredition donates a portion of the proceeds from each sold copy. As a reader of a TREDITION CLASSICS book, you support our mission to save many of the amazing works of world literature from oblivion. See all available books at www.tredition.com.

Project Gutenberg

The content for this book has been graciously provided by Project Gutenberg. Project Gutenberg is a non-profit organization founded by Michael Hart in 1971 at the University of Illinois. The mission of Project Gutenberg is simple: To encourage the creation and distribution of eBooks. Project Gutenberg is the first and largest collection of public domain eBooks.

The Rise of Iskander

Benjamin, Earl of Beaconsfield Disraeli

Imprint

This book is part of TREDITION CLASSICS

Author: Benjamin, Earl of Beaconsfield Disraeli
Cover design: Buchgut, Berlin – Germany

Publisher: tredition GmbH, Hamburg - Germany
ISBN: 978-3-8424-3204-8

www.tredition.com
www.tredition.de

The intention of the TREDITION CLASSICS series is to make world literature in the public domain available in printed format. Literary enthusiasts and organizations, such as Project Gutenberg, worldwide have scanned and digitally edited the original texts. tredition has subsequently formatted and redesigned the content into a modern reading layout. Therefore, we cannot guarantee the exact reproduction of the original format of a particular historic edition. Please also note that no modifications have been made to the spelling, therefore it may differ from the orthography used today.

THE RISE OF ISKANDER

By Benjamin Disraeli

Contents

CHAPTER 1

The sun had set behind the mountains, and the rich plain of Athens was suffused with the violet glow of a Grecian eye. A light breeze rose; the olive-groves awoke from their noonday trance, and rustled with returning animation, and the pennons of the Turkish squadron, that lay at anchor in the harbour of Piræus, twinkled in the lively air. From one gate of the city the women came forth in procession to the fountain; from another, a band of sumptuous horsemen sallied out, and threw their wanton javelins in the invigorating sky, as they galloped over the plain. The voice of birds, the buzz of beauteous insects, the breath of fragrant flowers, the quivering note of the nightingale, the pattering call of the grasshopper, and the perfume of the violet, shrinking from the embrace of the twilight breeze, filled the purple air with music and with odour.

A solitary being stood upon the towering crag of the Acropolis, amid the ruins of the Temple of Minerva, and gazed upon the inspiring scene. Around him rose the matchless memorials of antique art; immortal columns whose symmetry baffles modern proportion, serene Caryatides, bearing with greater grace a graceful burthen, carvings of delicate precision, and friezes breathing with heroic life. Apparently the stranger, though habited as a Moslemin, was not insensible to the genius of the locality, nor indeed would his form and countenance have misbecome a contemporary of Pericles and Phidias. In the prime of life and far above the common stature, but with a frame the muscular power of which was even exceeded by its almost ideal symmetry, white forehead, his straight profile, his oval countenance, and his curling lip, exhibited the same visage that had inspired the sculptor of the surrounding demigods.

The dress of the stranger, although gorgeous, was, however, certainly not classic. A crimson shawl was wound round his head and glittered with a trembling aigrette of diamonds. His vest which set tight to his form, was of green velvet, richly embroidered with gold and pearls. Over this he wore a very light jacket of crimson velvet, equally embroidered, and lined with sable. He wore also the full white camese common among the Albanians; and while his feet were protected by sandals, the lower part of his legs was guarded by greaves of embroidered green velvet. From a broad belt of scarlet leather peeped forth the jewelled hilts of a variety of daggers, and by his side was an enormous scimitar, in a scabbard of chased silver.

The stranger gazed upon the wide prospect before him with an air of pensive abstraction. "Beautiful Greece," he exclaimed, "thou art still my country. A mournful lot is mine, a strange and mournful lot, yet not uncheered by hope. I am at least a warrior; and this arm, though trained to war against thee, will not well forget, in the quick hour of battle, the blood that flows within it. Themistocles saved Greece and died a Satrap: I am bred one, let me reverse our lots, and die at least a patriot."

At this moment the Evening Hymn to the Virgin arose from a neighbouring convent. The stranger started as the sacred melody floated towards him, and taking a small golden cross from his heart, he kissed it with devotion, and then descending the steep of the citadel, entered the city.

He proceeded alone the narrow winding streets of Athens until he at length arrived in front of a marble palace, in the construction of which the architect had certainly not consulted the surrounding models which Time bad spared to him, but which, however, it might have offended a classic taste, presented altogether a magnificent appearance. Half-a-dozen guards, whose shields and helmets somewhat oddly contrasted with the two pieces of cannon, one of which was ostentatiously placed on each side of the portal, and which had been presented to the Prince of Athens by the Republic of Venice, lounged before the entrance, and paid their military homage to the stranger as he passed them. He passed them and entered a large quadrangular garden, surrounded by arcades, supported by a considerable number of thin, low pillars, of barbarous workmanship, and various-coloured marbles. In the midst of the garden rose a fountain, whence the bubbling waters flowed in artificial channels through vistas of orange and lemon trees. By the side of the fountain on a luxurious couch, his eyes fixed upon a richly-illuminated volume, reposed Nicæus, the youthful Prince of Athens.

"Ah! is it you?" said the Prince, looking up with a smile, as the stranger advanced. "You have arrived just in time to remind me that we must do something more than read the Persæ, we must act it."

"My dear Nicæus," replied the stranger, "I have arrived only to bid you farewell."

"Farewell!" exclaimed the Prince in a tone of surprise and sorrow; and he rose from the couch. "Why! what is this?"

"It is too true;" said the stranger, and he led the way down one of the walks. "Events have occurred which entirely baffle all our plans and prospects, and place me in a position as difficult as it is harrowing. Hunniades has suddenly crossed the Danube in great force, and carried everything before him. I am ordered to proceed to Albania instantly, and to repair to the camp at the head of the Epirots."

"Indeed!" said Nicæus, with a thoughtful air. "My letters did not prepare me for this. 'Tis sudden! Is Amurath himself in the field?"

"No; Karam Bey commands. I have accounted for my delay to the Sultan by pretended difficulties in our treaty, and have held out the prospect of a larger tribute."

"When we are plotting that that tribute should be paid no longer!" added Nicæus, with a smile.

"Alas! my dear friend," replied the Turkish commander, "my situation has now become critical. Hitherto my services for the Moslemin have been confined to acting against nations of their own faith. I am now suddenly summoned to combat against my secret creed, and the best allies of what I must yet call my secret country. The movement, it appears to me, must be made now or never, and I cannot conceal from myself, that it never could have been prosecuted under less auspicious circumstances."

"What, you desponding!" exclaimed Nicæus; "then I must despair. Your sanguine temper has alone supported me throughout all our dangerous hopes."

"And Æschylus?" said the stranger, smiling.

"And Æschylus, certainly," replied Nicæus; "but I have lived to find even Æschylus insipid. I pant for action."

"It may be nearer than we can foresee," replied the stranger. "There is a God who fashions all things. He will not desert a righteous cause. He knoweth that my thoughts are as pure as my situation is difficult. I have some dim ideas still brooding in my mind, but we will not discuss them now. I must away, dear Prince. The breeze serves fairly. Have you ever seen Hunniades?"

"I was educated at the Court of Transylvania," replied Nicæus, looking down with a somewhat embarrassed air. "He is a famous knight, Christendom's chief bulwark."

The Turkish commander sighed. "When we meet again," he said, "may we meet with brighter hopes and more buoyant spirits. At present, I must, indeed, say farewell."

The Prince turned with a dejected countenance, and pressed his companion to his heart. "'Tis a sad end," said he, "to all our happy hours and lofty plans."

"You are as yet too young to quarrel with Fortune," replied the stranger, "and for myself, I have not yet settled my accounts with her. However, for the present farewell, dear Nicæus!"

"Farewell," replied the Prince of Athens, "farewell, dear Iskander!"

CHAPTER 2

Iskander was the youngest son of the Prince of Epirus, who, with the other Grecian princes, had, at the commencement of the reign of Amurath the Second, in vain resisted the progress of the Turkish arms in Europe. The Prince of Epirus had obtained peace by yielding his four sons as hostages to the Turkish sovereign, who engaged that they should be educated in all the accomplishments of their rank, and with a due deference to their faith. On the death of the Prince of Epirus, however, Amurath could not resist the opportunity that then offered itself of adding to his empire the rich principality he had long coveted. A Turkish force instantly marched into Epirus, and seized upon Croia, the capital city, and the children of its late ruler were doomed to death. The beauty, talents, and valour of the youngest son, saved him, however, from the fate of his poisoned brothers. Iskander was educated at Adrianople, in the Moslemin faith, and as he, at a very early age, exceeded in feats of arms all the Moslemin warriors, he became a prime favourite of the Sultan, and speedily rose in his service to the highest rank.

At this period the irresistible progress of the Turkish arms was the subject of alarm throughout all Christendom.

Constantinople, then the capital of the Greek Empire, had already been more than once besieged by the predecessors of Amurath, and had only been preserved by fortunate accidents and humiliating terms. The despots of Bosnia, Servia, and Bulgaria, and the Grecian princes of Etolia, Macedon, Epirus, Athens, Phocis, Boeotia, and indeed of all the regions to the straits of Corinth, were tributaries to Amurath, and the rest of Europe was only preserved from his grasp by the valour of the Hungarians and the Poles, whom a fortunate alliance had now united under the sovereignty of Uladislaus, who, incited by the pious eloquence of the cardinal of St. Angelo, the legate of the Pope, and, yielding to the tears and supplications of the despot of Servia, had, at the time our story opens, quitted Buda, at the head of an immense army, crossed the Danube, and, joining his valiant viceroy, the famous John Hunniades, vaivode of Transylvania, defeated the Turks with great slaughter, relieved all Bulgaria, and pushed on to the base of Mount Hæmus, known in modern times as the celebrated Balkan. Here the Turkish general, Karam Bey, awaited the Christians, and hither to his assistance was Iskander commanded to repair at the head of a body of Janissaries, who had accompanied him to Greece, and the tributary Epirots.

Had Iskander been influenced by vulgar ambition, his loftiest desires might have been fully gratified by the career which Amurath projected for him. The Turkish Sultan destined for the Grecian Prince the hand of one of his daughters, and the principal command of his armies. He lavished upon him the highest dignities and boundless wealth; and, whether it arose from a feeling of remorse, or of affection for a warrior whose unexampled valour and unrivalled skill had already added some of the finest provinces of Asia to his rule, it is certain that Iskander might have exercised over Amurath a far greater degree of influence than was enjoyed by any other of his courtiers. But the heart of Iskander responded with no sympathy to these flattering favours. His Turkish education could never eradicate from his memory the consciousness that he was a Greek; and although he was brought up in the Moslemin faith, he had at an early period of his career, secretly recurred to the creed of his Christian fathers. He beheld in Amurath the murderer of his dearest kinsmen, and the oppressor of his country; and although a certain calmness of temper, and coolness of judgment, which very early developed themselves in his character, prevented him from ever giving any indication of his secret feelings, Iskander had long meditated on the exalted duty of freeing his country.

Dispatched to Greece, to arrange the tributes and the treaties of the Grecian princes, Iskander became acquainted with the young Nicæus; and their acquaintance soon matured into friendship. Nicæus was inexperienced; but nature had not intended him for action. The young Prince of Athens would loll by the side of a fountain, and dream of the wonders of old days. Surrounded by his eunuchs, his priests, and his courtiers, he envied Leonidas, and would have emulated Themistocles. He was passionately devoted to the ancient literature of his country, and had the good taste, rare at that time, to prefer Demosthenes and Lysias to Chrysostom and Gregory, and the choruses of the Grecian theatre to the hymns of the Greek church. The sustained energy and noble simplicity of the character of Iskander, seemed to recall to the young prince the classic heroes over whom he was so often musing, while the enthusiasm and fancy of Nicæus, and all that apparent weakness of will, and those quick vicissitudes of emotion, to which men of a fine susceptibility are subject, equally engaged the sympathy of the more vigorous and constant and experienced mind of his companion.

To Nicæus, Iskander had, for the first time in his life, confided much of his secret heart; and the young Prince fired at the inspiring tale. Often they consulted over the fortunes of their country, and, excited by their mutual invention, at length even dared to hope that they might effect its deliverance, when Iskander was summoned to the army. It was a mournful parting. Both of them felt that the last few months of their lives had owed many charms to their companionship. The parting of friends, united by sympathetic tastes, is always painful; and friends, unless this sympathy subsist, had much better never meet. Iskander stepped into the ship, sorrowful, but serene; Nicæus returned to his palace moody and fretful; lost his temper with his courtiers, and, when he was alone, even shed tears.

CHAPTER 3

Three weeks bad elapsed since the parting of Iskander and Nicæus, when the former, at the head of ten thousand men, entered by a circuitous route the defiles of Mount Hæmus, and approached the Turkish camp, which had been pitched, upon a vast and elevated table-ground, commanded on all sides by superior heights, which, however, were fortified and well-garrisoned by Janissaries. The Epirots halted, and immediately prepared to raise their tents, while their commander, attended by a few of his officers, instantly proceeded to the pavilion of Karam Bey.

The arrival of Iskander diffused great joy among the soldiery; and as he passed through the encampment, the exclamations of the Turkish warriors announced how ready they were to be led to the charge by a chieftain who had been ever successful. A guard of honour, by the orders of Karam Bey, advanced to conduct Iskander to his presence; and soon, entering the pavilion, the Grecian prince exchanged courtesies with the Turkish general. After the formal compliments had passed, Karam Bey waved his hand, and the pavilion was cleared, with the exception of Mousa, the chief secretary, and favourite of Karam.

"You have arrived in good time, Iskander, to assist in the destruction of the Christian dogs," said the Bey. "Flushed with their accursed success, they have advanced too far. Twice they have endeavoured to penetrate the mountains; and each time they have been forced to retire, with great loss. The passages are well barricadoed with timber and huge fragments of rock. The dogs have lost all heart, and are sinking under the joint sufferings of hunger and cold. Our scouts tell me they exhibit symptoms of retreat. We must rush down from the mountains, and annihilate them."

"Is Hunniades here in person?" inquired Iskander.

"He is here," replied Karam, "in person, the dog of dogs! Come, Iskander, his head would be a fine Ramadan present to Amurath. 'Tis a head worth three tails, I guess."

Mousa, the chief secretary, indulged in some suppressed laughter at this joke. Iskander smiled.

"If they retreat we must assuredly attack them," observed Iskander, musingly. "I have a persuasion that Hunniades and myself will soon meet."

"If there be truth in the Prophet!" exclaimed Karam. "I have no doubt of it. Hunniades is reserved for you, Bey. We shall hold up our heads at court yet, Iskander. You have had letters lately?"

"Some slight words."

"No mention of us, of course?"

"Nothing, except some passing praise of your valour and discretion."

"We do our best, we do our best. Will Isa Bey have Ætolia, think you?"

"I have no thoughts. Our royal father will not forget his children, and Isa Bey is a most valiant chieftain."

"You heard not that he was coming here?" inquired Karam.

"Have you?" responded the cautious Iskander.

"A rumour, a rumour," replied Karam. "He is at Adrianople, think you?"

"It may be so: I am, you know, from Athens."

"True, true. We shall beat them, Iskander, we shall beat them."

"For myself, I feel sanguine," replied the Prince, and he arose to retire. "I must at present to my men. We must ascertain more accurately the movements of the Christians before we decide on our own. I am inclined myself to reconnoitre them. How far may it be?"

"There is not room to form our array between them and the mountains," replied Karam.

"'Tis well. Success attend the true believers! By to-morrow's dawn we shall know more."

CHAPTER 4

Iskander returned to his men. Night was coming on. Fires and lights blazed and sparkled in every direction. The air was clear, but very cold. He entered his tent, and muffling himself up in his pelisse of sables, he mounted his horse, and declining any attendance, rode for some little distance, until he had escaped from the precincts of the camp. Then he turned his horse towards one of the wildest passes of the mountain, and galloping at great speed, never stopped until he had gained a considerable ascent. The track became steep and rugged. The masses of loose stone rendered his progress slow; but his Anatolian charger still bore him at intervals bravely, and in three hours' time he had gained the summit of Mount Hæmus. A brilliant moon flooded the broad plains of Bulgaria with shadowy light. At the base of the mountainous range, the red watch-fires denoted the situation of the Christian camp.

Iskander proceeded down the descent with an audacious rapidity; but his charger was thorough-bred, and his moments were golden. Ere midnight, he had reached the outposts of the enemy, and was challenged by a sentinel.

"Who goes there?"

"A friend to Christendom."

"The word?"

"I have it not—nay calmly. I am alone, but I am not unarmed. I do not know the word. I come from a far country, and bear important tidings to the great Hunniades; conduct me to that chief."

"May I be crucified if I will," responded the sentinel, "before I know who and what you are. Come, keep off, unless you wish to try the effect of a Polish lance," continued the sentinel; "'tis something, I assure you, not less awkward than your Greek fire, if Greek indeed you be."

"My friend, you are a fool," said Iskander, "but time is too precious to argue any longer." So saying, the Turkish commander dismounted, and taking up the brawny sentinel in his arms with the greatest ease, threw him over his shoulder, and threatening the astounded soldier with instant death if he struggled, covered him with his pelisse, and entered the camp.

They approached a watch-fire, around which several soldiers were warming themselves.

"Who goes there?" inquired a second sentinel.

"A friend to Christendom," answered Iskander.

"The word?"

Iskander hesitated.

"The word, or I'll let fly," said the sentinel, elevating his cross bow.

"The Bridge of Buda," instantly replied the terrified prisoner beneath the pelisse of Iskander.

"Why did not you answer before, then?" said one of the guards.

"And why do you mock us by changing your voice?" said another. "Come, get on with you, and no more jokes."

Iskander proceeded through a street of tents, in some of which were lights, but all of which were silent. At length, he met the esquire of a Polish knight returning from a convivial meeting, not a little elevated.

"Who are you?" inquired Iskander.

"I am an Esquire," replied the gentleman.

"A shrewd man, I doubt not, who would make his fortune," replied Iskander. "You must know great things have happened. Being on guard I have taken a prisoner, who has deep secrets to divulge to the Lord Hunniades. Thither, to his pavilion, I am now bearing him. But he is a stout barbarian, and almost too much for me. Assist me in carrying him to the pavilion of Hunniades, and you shall have all the reward, and half the fame."

"You are a very civil spoken young gentleman," said the Esquire. "I think I know your voice. Your name, if I mistake not, is Leckinski?"

"A relative. We had a common ancestor."

"I thought so. I know the Leckinskies ever by their voice. I am free to help you on the terms you mention—all the reward and half the fame. 'Tis a strong barbarian, is it? We cannot cut his throat, or it will not divulge. All the reward and half the fame! I will be a knight to-morrow. It seems a sort of fish, and has a smell."

The Esquire seized the Shoulders of the prisoner, who would have spoken had he not been terrified by the threats of Iskander, who, carrying the legs of the sentinel, allowed the Polish gentleman to lead the way to the pavilion of Hunniades. Thither they soon arrived; and Iskander, dropping his burthen, and leaving the prisoner without to the charge of his assistant, entered the pavilion of the General of the Hungarians.

He was stopped in a small outer apartment by an officer, who inquired his purpose, and to whom he repeated his desire to see the Hungarian leader, without loss of time, on important business. The officer hesitated; but, summoning several guards, left Iskander in their custody, and, stepping behind a curtain, disappeared. Iskander heard voices, but could distinguish no words. Soon the officer returned, and, ordering the guards to disarm and search Iskander, directed the Grecian Prince to follow him. Drawing aside the curtain, Iskander and his attendant entered a low apartment of considerable size. It was hung with skins. A variety of armour and dresses were piled on couches. A middle-aged man, of majestic appearance, muffled in a pelisse of furs, with long chestnut hair, and a cap of crimson velvet and ermine, was walking up and down the apartment, and dictating some instructions to a person who was kneeling on the ground, and writing by the bright flame of a brazen lamp. The bright flame of the blazing lamp fell full upon the face of the secretary. Iskander beheld a most beautiful woman.

She looked up as Iskander entered. Her large dark eyes glanced through his soul. Her raven hair descended to her shoulders in many curls on each side of her face, and was braided with strings of immense pearls. A broad cap of white fox-skin crowned her whiter forehead. Her features were very small, but sharply moulded, and a delicate tint gave animation to her clear fair cheek. She looked up as Iskander entered, with an air rather of curiosity than embarrassment.

Hunniades stopped, and examined his visitor with a searching inquisition. "Whence come you?" inquired the Hungarian chieftain.

"From the Turkish camp," was the answer.

"An envoy or a deserter?"

"Neither."

"What then?"

"A convert."

"Your name?"

"Lord Hunniades," said Iskander, "that is for your private ear. I am unarmed, and were I otherwise, the first knight of Christendom can scarcely fear. I am one in birth and rank your equal; if not in fame, at least, I trust, in honour. My time is all-precious: I can scarcely stay here while my horse breathes. Dismiss your attendant."

Hunniades darted a glance at his visitor which would have baffled a weaker brain, but Iskander stood the scrutiny calm and undisturbed. "Go, Stanislaus," said the Vaivode to the officer. "This lady, sir," continued the chieftain, "is my daughter, and one from whom I have no secrets."

Iskander bowed lowly as the officer disappeared.

"And now," said Hunniades, "to business. Your purpose?"

"I am a Grecian Prince, and a compulsory ally of the Moslemin. In a word, my purpose here is to arrange a plan by which we may effect, at the same time, your triumph, and my freedom."

"To whom, then, have I the honour of speaking?" inquired Hunniades.

"My name, great Hunniades, is perhaps not altogether unknown to you: they call me Iskander."

"What, the right arm of Amurath, the conqueror of Caramania, the flower of Turkish chivalry? Do I indeed behold that matchless warrior?" exclaimed Hunniades, and he held forth his hand to his guest, and ungirding his own sword, offered it to the Prince. "Iduna" continued Hunniades, to his daughter, "you at length behold Iskander."

"My joy is great, sir," replied Iduna, "if I indeed rightly understand that we may count the Prince Iskander a champion of the Cross."

Iskander took from his heart his golden crucifix, and kissed it before her. "This has been my companion and consolation for long years, lady," said Iskander; "you, perhaps, know my mournful history, Hunniades. Hitherto my pretended sovereign has not required me to bare my scimitar against my Christian brethren. That hour, however, has at length arrived, and it has decided me to adopt a line of conduct long meditated. Karam Bey who is aware of your necessities, the moment you commence your retreat, will attack you. I shall command his left wing. In spite of his superior power and position, draw up in array, and meet him with confidence. I propose, at a convenient moment in the day, to withdraw my troops, and with the Epirots hasten to my native country, and at once raise the standard of independence. It is a bold measure, but Success is the child of Audacity. We must assist each other with mutual diversions. Single-handed it is in vain for me to commence a struggle, which, with all adventitious advantages, will require the utmost exertion of energy, skill, and patience. But if yourself and the King Uladislaus occupy the armies of Amurath in Bulgaria, I am not without hope of ultimate success, since I have to inspire me all the most urgent interests of humanity, and combat, at the same time, for my God, my country, and my lawful crown."

"Brave Prince, I pledge you my troth," said Hunniades, coming forward and seizing his hand; "and while Iskander and Hunniades live, they will never cease until they have achieved their great and holy end."

"It is a solemn compact," said Iskander, "more sacred than if registered by all the scribes of Christendom. Lady Iduna, your prayers!"

"They are ever with the champions of the Cross," replied the daughter of Hunniades. She rose, the large cloak in which she was enveloped fell from her exquisite form. "Noble Iskander, this rosary is from the Holy Sepulchre," continued Iduna; "wear it for the sake and memory of that blessed Saviour who died for our sins."

Iskander held forth his arm and touched her delicate hand as he received the rosary, which, pressing to his lips, he placed round his neck.

"Great Hunniades," said the Grecian Prince, "I must cross the mountains before dawn. Let me venture to entreat that we should hear to-morrow that the Christian camp is in retreat."

"Let it be even so," said the Hungarian, after some thought, "and may to-morrow's sun bring brighter days to Christendom." And with these words terminated the brief and extraordinary visit of Iskander to the Christian general.

CHAPTER 5

The intelligence of the breaking up of the Christian camp, and the retreat of the Christian army, soon reached the Divan of Karam Bey, who immediately summoned Iskander to consult on the necessary operations. The chieftains agreed that instant pursuit was indispensable, and soon the savage Hæmus poured forth from its green bosom swarms of that light cavalry which was perhaps even a more fatal arm of the Turkish power than the famous Janissaries themselves. They hovered on the rear of the retreating Christians, charged the wavering, captured the unwary. It was impossible to resist their sudden and impetuous movements, which rendered their escape as secure as their onset was overwhelming. Wearied at length by the repeated assaults, Hunniades, who, attended by some chosen knights, had himself repaired to the rear, gave orders for the army to halt and offer battle.

Their pursuers instantly withdrew to a distance, and gradually forming into two divisions, awaited the arrival of the advancing army of the Turks. The Moslemin came forward in fierce array, and with the sanguine courage inspired by expected triumph. Very conspicuous was Iskander bounding in his crimson vest upon his ebon steed and waving his gleaming scimitar.

The Janissaries charged, calling upon Allah! with an awful shout. The Christian knights, invoking the Christian saints, received the Turks at the points of their lances. But many a noble lance was shivered that morn, and many a bold rider and worthy steed bit the dust of that field, borne down by the irresistible numbers of their fierce adversaries. Everywhere the balls and the arrows whistled through the air, and sometimes an isolated shriek heard amid the general clang, announced another victim to the fell and mysterious agency of the Greek fire.

Hunniades, while he performed all the feats of an approved warrior, watched with anxiety the disposition of the Turkish troops. Hitherto, from the nature of their position, but a portion of both armies had interfered in the contest, and as yet Iskander had kept aloof. But now, as the battle each instant raged with more fury, and as it was evident that ere long the main force of both armies must be brought into collision, Hunniades, with a terrible suspense, watched whether the Grecian prince were willing or even capable of executing his plan. Without this fulfilment, the Christian hero could not conceal from himself that the day must be decided against the Cross.

In the meantime Iskander marked the course of events with not less eagerness than Hunniades. Already Karam Bey had more than once summoned him to bring the Epirots into action. He assented; but an hour passed away without changing his position. At length, more from astonishment than rage, the Turkish commander sent his chief secretary Mousa himself to impress his wishes upon his colleague, and obtain some explanation of his views and conduct. Mousa found Iskander surrounded by some of the principal Epirot nobles, all mounted on horseback, and standing calmly under a wide-spreading plane tree. The chief secretary of Karam Bey was too skilful a courtier to permit his countenance to express his feelings, and he delivered himself of a mission rather as if he had come to request advice, than to communicate a reprimand.

"Your master is a wise man, Mousa," replied Iskander; "but even Karam Bey may be mistaken. He deems that a battle is not to be won by loitering under a shadowy tree. Now I differ with him, and I even mean to win this day by such a piece of truancy. However, it may certainly now be time for more active work. You smile encouragement, good Mousa. Giorgio, Demetrius, to your duty!"

At these words, two stout Epirots advanced to the unfortunate secretary, seized and bound him, and placed him on horseback before one of their comrades.

"Now all who love their country follow me!" exclaimed Iskander. So saying, and at the head of five thousand horsemen, Iskander quitted the field at a rapid pace.

CHAPTER 6

With incredible celerity Iskander and his cavalry dashed over the plains of Roumelia, and never halted, except for short and hurried intervals of rest and repose, until they had entered the mountainous borders of Epirus, and were within fifty miles of its capital, Croia. On the eve of entering the kingdom of his fathers, Iskander ordered his guards to produce the chief secretary of Karam Bey. Exhausted with fatigue, vexation, and terror, the disconsolate Mousa was led forward.

"Cheer up, worthy Mousa!" said Iskander, lying his length on the green turf. "We have had a sharp ride; but I doubt not we shall soon find ourselves, by the blessing of God, in good quarters. There is a city at hand which they call Croia, and in which once, as the rumour runs, the son of my father should not have had to go seek for an entrance. No matter. Methinks, worthy Mousa, thou art the only man in our society that can sign thy name. Come now, write me an order signed Karam Bey to the governor of this said city, for its delivery up to the valiant champion of the Crescent, Iskander, and thou shalt ride in future at a pace more suitable to a secretary."

The worthy Mousa humbled himself to the ground, and then talking his writing materials from his girdle, inscribed the desired order, and delivered it to Iskander, who, glancing at the inscription, pushed it into his vest.

"I shall proceed at once to Croia, with a few friends," said Iskander; "do you, my bold companions, follow me this eve in various parties, and in various routes. At dead of the second night, collect in silence before the gates of Croia!"

Thus speaking, Iskander called for his now refreshed charger, and, accompanied by two hundred horsemen, bade farewell for a brief period to his troops, and soon having crossed the mountains, descended into the fertile plains of Epirus.

When the sun rose in the morning, Iskander and his friends beheld at the further end of the plain a very fine city shining in the light. It was surrounded with lofty turreted walls flanked by square towers, and was built upon a gentle eminence, which gave it a very majestic appearance. Behind it rose a lofty range of purple mountains of very picturesque form, and the highest peaks capped with snow. A noble lake, from which troops of wild fowl occasionally rose, expanded like a sheet of silver on one side of the city. The green breast of the contiguous hills sparkled with white houses.

"Behold Croia!" exclaimed Iskander. "Our old fathers could choose a site, comrades. We shall see whether they expended their time and treasure for strangers, or their own seed." So saying, he spurred his horse, and with panting hearts and smiling faces, Iskander and his company had soon arrived in the vicinity of the city.

The city was surrounded by a beautiful region of corn-fields and fruit-trees. The road was arched with the over-hanging boughs. The birds chirped on every spray. It was a blithe and merry morn. Iskander plucked a bunch of olives as he cantered along. "Dear friends," he said, looking round with an inspiring smile, "let us gather our first harvest!" And, thereupon, each putting forth his rapid hand, seized, as he rushed by, the emblem of possession, and following the example of his leader, placed it in his cap.

They arrived at the gates of the city, which was strongly garrisoned; and Iskander, followed by his train, galloped up the height of the citadel. Alighting from his horse, he was ushered into the divan of the governor, an ancient Pacha, who received the conqueror of Caramania with all the respect that became so illustrious a champion of the Crescent. After the usual forms of ceremonious hospitality, Iskander, with a courteous air presented him the order for delivering up the citadel; and the old Pacha, resigning himself to the loss of his post with Oriental submission, instantly delivered the keys of the citadel and town to Iskander, and requested permission immediately to quit the scene of his late command.

Quitting the citadel, Iskander now proceeded through the whole town, and in the afternoon reviewed the Turkish garrison in the great square. As the late governor was very anxious to quit Croia that very day, Iskander insisted on a considerable portion of the garrison accompanying him as a guard of honour, and returning the next morning. The rest he divided in several quarters, and placed the gates in charge of his own companions.

At midnight the Epirots, faithful to their orders, arrived and united beneath the walls of the city, and after inter-changing the signals agreed upon, the gates were opened. A large body instantly marched and secured the citadel. The rest, conducted by appointed leaders, surrounded the Turks in their quarters. And suddenly, in the noon of night, in that great city, arose a clang so dreadful that people leapt up from their sleep and stared with stupor. Instantly the terrace of every house blazed with torches, and it became as light as day. Troops of armed men were charging down the streets, brandishing their scimitars and yataghans, and exclaiming, "The Cross, the Cross!" "Liberty!" "Greece!" "Iskander and Epirus!" The townsmen recognised their countrymen by their language and their dress. The name of Iskander acted as a spell. They stopt not to inquire. A magic sympathy at once persuaded them that this great man had, by the grace of Heaven, recurred to the creed and country of his fathers. And so every townsman, seizing the nearest weapon, with a spirit of patriotic frenzy, rushed into the streets, crying out, "The Cross, the Cross!" "Liberty!" "Greece!" "Iskander and Epirus!" Ay! even the women lost all womanly fears, and stimulated instead of soothing the impulse of their masters. They fetched them arms, they held the torches, they sent them forth with vows and prayers and imprecations, their children clinging to their robes, and repeating with enthusiasm, phrases which they could not comprehend.

The Turks fought with the desperation of men who feel that they are betrayed, and must be victims. The small and isolated bodies were soon massacred, all with cold steel, for at this time, although some of the terrible inventions of modern warfare were introduced, their use was not general. The citadel, indeed, was fortified with cannon; but the greater part of the soldiery trusted to their crooked swords, and their unerring javelins. The main force of the Turkish garrison had been quartered in an old palace of the Archbishop, situate in the middle of the city on a slightly rising and open ground, a massy building of rustic stone. Here the Turks, although surrounded, defended themselves desperately, using their cross bows with terrible effect; and hither, the rest of the city being now secured, Iskander himself repaired to achieve its complete deliverance.

The Greeks had endeavoured to carry the principal entrance of the palace by main force, but the strength of the portal had resisted their utmost exertions, and the arrows of the besieged had at length forced them to retire to a distance. Iskander directed that two pieces of cannon should be dragged down from the citadel, and then played against the entrance. In the meantime, he ordered immense piles of damp faggots to be lit before the building, the smoke of which prevented the besieged from taking any aim. The ardour of the people was so great that the cannon were soon served against the palace, and their effects were speedily remarked. The massy portal shook; a few blows of the battering ram, and it fell. The Turks sallied forth, were received with a shower of Greek fire, and driven in with agonising yells. Some endeavoured to escape from the windows, and were speared or cut down; some appeared wringing their hands in despair upon the terraced roof. Suddenly the palace was announced to be on fire. A tall white-blueish flame darted up from a cloud of smoke, and soon, as if by magic, the whole back of the building was encompassed with rising tongues of red and raging light. Amid a Babel of shrieks, and shouts, and cheers, and prayers, and curses, the roof of the palace fell in with a crash, which produced amid the besiegers an awful and momentary silence, but in an instant they started from their strange inactivity, and rushing forward, leapt into the smoking ruins, and at the same time completed the massacre and achieved their freedom.

CHAPTER 7

At break of dawn Iskander sent couriers throughout all Epirus, announcing the fall of Croia, and that he had raised the standard of independence in his ancient country. He also despatched a trusty messenger to Prince Nicæus at Athens, and to the great Hunniades. The people were so excited throughout all Epirus, at this great and unthought-of intelligence, that they simultaneously rose in all the open country, and massacred the Turks, and the towns were only restrained in a forced submission to Amurath, by the strong garrisons of the Sultan.

Now Iskander was very anxious to effect the removal of these garrisons without loss of time, in order that if Amurath sent a great power against him, as he expected, the invading army might have nothing to rely upon but its own force, and that his attention might not in any way be diverted from effecting their overthrow. Therefore, as soon as his troops had rested, and he had formed his new recruits into some order, which, with their willing spirits, did not demand many days, Iskander set out from Croia, at the head of twelve thousand men, and marched against the strong city of Petrella, meeting in his way the remainder of the garrison of Croia on their return, who surrendered themselves to him at discretion. Petrella was only one day's march from Croia, and when Iskander arrived there he requested a conference with the governor, and told his tale so well, representing the late overthrow of the Turks by Hunniades, and the incapacity of Amurath at present to relieve him, that the Turkish commander agreed to deliver up the place, and leave the country with his troops, particularly as the alternative of Iskander to these easy terms was ever conquest without quarter. And thus, by a happy mixture of audacity and adroitness, the march of Iskander throughout Epirus was rather like a triumph than a campaign, the Turkish garrisons imitating, without any exception, the conduct of their comrades at Petrella, and dreading the fate of their comrades at the capital. In less than a month Iskander returned to Epirus, having delivered the whole country from the Moslemin yoke.

Hitherto Iskander had heard nothing either of Hunniades or Nicæus. He learnt, therefore, with great interest, as he passed through the gates of the city, that the Prince of Athens had arrived at Croia the preceding eve, and also that his messenger had returned from the Hungarian camp. Amid the acclamations of an enthusiastic people, Iskander once more ascended the citadel of Croia. Nicæus received him at the gate. Iskander sprang from his horse, and embraced his friend. Hand in hand, and followed by their respective trains, they entered the fortress palace.

"Dear friend," said Iskander, when they were once more alone, "you see we were right not to despair. Two months have scarcely elapsed since we parted without prospect, or with the most gloomy one, and now we are in a fair way of achieving all that we can desire. Epirus is free!"

"I came to claim my share in its emancipation," said Nicæus, with a smile, "but Iskander is another Cæsar!"

"You will have many opportunities yet, believe me, Nicæus, of proving your courage and your patriotism," replied Iskander; "Amurath will never allow this affair to pass over in this quiet manner. I did not commence this struggle without a conviction that it would demand all the energy and patience of a long life. I shall be rewarded if I leave freedom as an heritage to my countrymen; but for the rest, I feel that I bid farewell to every joy of life, except the ennobling consciousness of performing a noble duty. In the meantime, I understand a messenger awaits me here from the great Hunniades. Unless that shield of Christendom maintain himself in his present position, our chance of ultimate security is feeble. With his constant diversion in Bulgaria, we may contrive here to struggle into success. You sometimes laugh at my sanguine temper, Nicæus. To say the truth, I am more serene than sanguine, and was never more conscious of the strength of my opponent than now, when it appears that I have beaten him. Hark! the people cheer. I love the people, Nicæus, who are ever influenced by genuine and generous feelings. They cheer as if they had once more gained a country. Alas! they little know what they must endure even at the best. Nay! look not gloomy; we have done great things, and will do more. Who waits without there? Demetrius! Call the messenger from Lord Hunniades."

An Epirot bearing a silken packet was now introduced, which he delivered to Iskander. Reverently touching the hand of his chieftain, the messenger then kissed his own and withdrew. Iskander broke the seal, and drew forth a letter from the silken cover.

"So! this is well!" exclaimed the prince, with great animation, as he threw his quick eye over the letter. "As I hoped and deemed, a most complete victory. Karam Bey himself a prisoner, baggage, standards, great guns, treasure. Brave soldier of the Cross! (may I prove so!) Your perfectly-devised movement, (poh, poh!) Hah! what is this?" exclaimed Iskander, turning pale; his lip quivered, his eye looked dim. He walked to an arched window. His companion, who supposed that he was reading, did not disturb him.

"Poor, poor Hunniades!" at length exclaimed Iskander, shaking his head.

"What of him?" inquired Nicæus, quickly.

"The sharpest accident of war!" replied Iskander. "It quite clouds my spirit. We must forget these things, we must forget. Epirus! he is not a patriot who can spare a thought from thee. And yet, so young, so beautiful, so gifted, so worthy of a hero! when I saw her by her great father's side, sharing his toils, aiding his councils, supplying his necessities, methought I gazed upon a ministering angel! upon—"

"Stop, stop in mercy's name, Iskander!" exclaimed Nicæus, in a very agitated tone. "What is all this? Surely no, surely not, surely Iduna—"

"'Tis she!"

"Dead?" exclaimed Nicæus, rushing up to his companion, and seizing his arm.

"Worse, much worse!"

"God of Heaven!" exclaimed the young Prince, with almost a frantic air. "Tell me all, tell me all! This suspense fires my brain. Iskander, you know not what this woman is to me; the sole object of my being, the bane, the blessing of my life! Speak, dear friend, speak! I beseech you! Where is Iduna?"

"A prisoner to the Turk."

"Iduna a prisoner to the Turk. I'll not believe it! Why do we wear swords? Where's chivalry? Iduna, a prisoner to the Turk! 'Tis false. It cannot be. Iskander, you are a coward! I am a coward! All are cowards! A prisoner to the Turk! Iduna! What, the Rose of Christendom! has it been plucked by such a turbaned dog as Amurath? Farewell, Epirus! Farewell, classic Athens! Farewell, bright fields of Greece, and dreams that made them brighter! The sun of all my joy and hope is set, and set for ever!"

So saying, Nicæus, tearing his hair and garments, flung himself upon the floor, and hid his face in his robes.

Iskander paced the room with a troubled step and thoughtful brow. After some minutes he leant down by the Prince of Athens, and endeavoured to console him.

"It is in vain, Iskander, it is in vain," said Nicæus. "I wish to die."

"Were I a favoured lover, in such a situation," replied Iskander, "I should scarcely consider death my duty, unless the sacrifice of myself preserved my mistress."

"Hah!" exclaimed Nicæus, starting from the ground. "Do you conceive, then, the possibility of rescuing her?"

"If she live, she is a prisoner in the Seraglio at Adrianople. You are as good a judge as myself of the prospect that awaits your exertions. It is, without doubt, a difficult adventure, but such, methinks, as a Christian knight should scarcely shun."

"To horse;" exclaimed Nicæus, "to horse—And yet what can I do? Were she in any other place but the capital I might rescue her by force, but in the heart of their empire, it is impossible. Is there no ransom that can tempt the Turk? My principality would rise in the balance beside this jewel."

"That were scarcely wise, and certainly not just," replied Iskander; "but ransom will be of no avail. Hunniades has already offered to restore Karam Bey, and all the prisoners of rank, and the chief trophies, and Amurath has refused to listen to any terms. The truth is,

Iduna has found favour in the eyes of his son, the young Mahomed."

"Holy Virgin! hast thou no pity on this Christian maid?" exclaimed Nicæus. "The young Mahomed! Shall this licentious infidel—ah! Iskander, dear, dear Iskander, you who have so much wisdom, and so much courage; you who can devise all things, and dare all things; help me, help me; on my knees I do beseech you, take up this trying cause of foul oppression, and for the sake of all you love and reverence, your creed, your country, and perchance your friend, let your great genius, like some solemn angel, haste to the rescue of the sweet Iduna, and save her, save her!"

"Some thoughts like these were rising in my mind when first I spoke," replied Iskander. "This is a better cue, far more beseeming princes than boyish tears, and all the outward misery of woe, a tattered garment and dishevelled locks. Come, Nicæus, we have to struggle with a mighty fortune. Let us be firm as Fate itself."

CHAPTER 8

Immediately after his interview with Nicæus, Iskander summoned some of the chief citizens of Croia to the citadel, and submitting to them his arrangements for the administration of Epirus, announced the necessity of his instant departure for a short interval; and the same evening, ere the moon had risen, himself and the Prince of Athens quitted the city, and proceeded in the direction of Adrianople. They travelled with great rapidity until they reached a small town upon the frontiers, where they halted for one day. Here, in the Bazaar, Iskander purchased for himself the dress of an Armenian physician. In his long dark robes, and large round cap of black wool, his face and hands stained, and his beard and mustachios shaven, it seemed impossible that he could be recognised. Nicæus was habited as his page, in a dress of coarse red cloth, setting tight to his form, with a red cap, with a long blue tassel. He carried a large bag containing drugs, some surgical instruments, and a few books. In this guise, as soon as the gates were open on the morrow, Iskander, mounted on a very small mule, and Nicæus on a very large donkey, the two princes commenced the pass of the mountainous range, an arm of the Balkan which divided Epirus from Roumelia.

"I broke the wind of the finest charger in all Asia when I last ascended these mountains," said Iskander; "I hope this day's journey way be accepted as a sort of atonement."

"Faith! there is little doubt I am the best mounted of the two," said Nicæus. "However, I hope we shall return at a sharper pace."

"How came it, my Nicæus," said Iskander, "that you never mentioned to me the name of Iduna when we were at Athens? I little supposed when I made my sudden visit to Hunniades, that I was about to appeal to so fair a host. She is a rarely gifted lady."

"I knew of her being at the camp as little as yourself," replied the Prince of Athens, "and for the rest, the truth is, Iskander, there are some slight crosses in our loves, which Time, I hope, will fashion rightly." So saying Nicæus pricked on his donkey, and flung his stick at a bird which was perched on the branch of a tree. Iskander did not resume a topic to which his companion seemed disinclined. Their journey was tedious. Towards nightfall they reached the summit of the usual track; and as the descent was difficult, they were obliged to rest until daybreak.

On the morrow they had a magnificent view of the rich plains of Roumelia, and in the extreme distance, the great city of Adrianople, its cupolas and minarets blazing and sparkling in the sun. This glorious prospect at once revived all their energies. It seemed that the moment of peril and of fate had arrived. They pricked on their sorry steeds; and on the morning of the next day, presented themselves at the gates of the city. The thorough knowledge which Iskander possessed of the Turkish character obtained them an entrance, which was at one time almost doubtful, from the irritability and impatience of Nicæus. They repaired to a caravansera of good repute in the neighbourhood of the seraglio; and having engaged their rooms, the Armenian physician, attended by his page, visited several of the neighbouring coffee-houses, announcing, at the same time, his arrival, his profession, and his skill.

As Iskander felt pulses, examined tongues, and distributed drugs and charms, he listened with interest and amusement to the conversation of which he himself was often the hero. He found that the Turks had not yet recovered from their consternation at his audacity and success. They were still wondering, and if possible more astounded than indignant. The politicians of the coffee-houses, chiefly consisting of Janissaries, were loud in their murmurs. The popularity of Amurath had vanished before the triumph of Hunniades, and the rise of Iskander.

"But Allah has in some instances favoured the faithful," remarked Iskander; "I heard in my travels of your having captured a great princess of the Giaours."

"God is great!" said an elderly Turk with a long white heard. "The Hakim congratulates the faithful because they have taken a woman!"

"Not so merely," replied Iskander; "I heard the woman was a princess. If so, the people of Franguestan will pay any ransom for their great women; and, by giving up this fair Giaour, you may free many of the faithful."

"Mashallah!" said another ancient Turk, sipping his coffee. "The Hakim speaks wisely."

"May I murder my mother!" exclaimed a young Janissary, with great indignation. "But this is the very thing that makes me wild against Amurath. Is not this princess a daughter of that accursed Giaour, that dog of dogs, Hunniades? and has he not offered for her ransom our brave Karam Bey himself, and his chosen warriors? and has not Amurath said nay? And why has he said nay? Because his son, the Prince of Mahomed, instead of fighting against the Giaours, has looked upon one of their women, and has become a Mejnoun. Pah! May I murder my mother, but if the Giaours were in full march to the city, I'd not fight. And let him tell this to the Cadi who dares; for there are ten thousand of us, and we have sworn by the Kettle but we will not fight for Giaours, or those who love Giaours!"

"If you mean me, Ali, about going to the Cadi," said the chief eunuch of Mahomed, who was standing by, "let me tell you I am no tale-bearer, and scorn to do an unmanly act. The young prince can beat the Giaours without the aid of those who are noisy enough in a coffee-house when they are quiet enough in the field. And, for the rest of the business, you may all ease your hearts; for the Frangy princess you talk of is pining away, and will soon die. The Sultan has offered a hundred purses of gold to any one who cures her; but the gold will never be counted by the Hasnadar, or I will double it."

"Try your fortune, Hakim," said several laughing loungers to Iskander.

"Allah has stricken the Frangy princess," said the old Turk with a white beard.

"He will strike all Giaours," said his ancient companion, sipping his coffee. "It is so written."

"Well! I do not like to hear of women slaves pining to death," said the young Janissary, in a softened tone, "particularly when they are young. Amurath should have ransomed her, or he might have given her to one of his officers, or any young fellow that had particularly distinguished himself." And so, twirling his mustachios, and flinging down his piastre, the young Janissary strutted out of the coffee-house.

"When we were young," said the old Turk with the white beard to his companion, shaking his head, "when we were young— "

"We conquered Anatolia, and never opened our mouths," rejoined his companion.

"I never offered an opinion till I was sixty," said the old Turk; "and then it was one which had been in our family for a century."

"No wonder Hunniades carries everything before him," said his companion.

"And that accursed Iskander," said the old man.

The chief eunuch, finishing his vase of sherbet, moved away. The Armenian physician followed him.

CHAPTER 9

The chief eunuch turned into a burial-ground, through which a way led, by an avenue of cypress-trees, to the quarter of the Seraglio. The Armenian physician, accompanied by his page, followed him.

"Noble sir!" said the Armenian physician; "may I trespass for a moment on your lordship's attention?"

"Worthy Hakim, is it you?" replied the chief eunuch, turning round with an encouraging smile of courteous condescension, "your pleasure?"

"I would speak to you of important matters," said the physician.

The eunuch carelessly seated himself on a richly-carved tomb, and crossing his legs with an air of pleasant superiority, adjusted a fine emerald that sparkled on his finger, and bade the Hakim address him without hesitation.

"I am a physician," said the Armenian.

The eunuch nodded.

"And I heard your lordship in the coffee-house mention that the Sultan, our sublime Master, had offered a rich reward to any one who could effect the cure of a favourite captive."

"No less a reward than one hundred purses of gold," remarked the eunuch. "The reward is proportioned to the exigency of the cue. Believe me, worthy sir, it is desperate."

"With mortal means," replied the Armenian; "but I possess a talisman of magical influence, which no disorder can resist. I would fain try its efficacy."

"This is not the first talisman that has been offered us, worthy doctor," said the eunuch, smiling incredulously.

"But the first that has been offered on these terms," said the Armenian. "Let me cure the captive, and of the one hundred purses, a moiety shall belong to yourself. Ay! so confident am I of success, that I deem it no hazard to commence our contract by this surety."

And so saying, the Armenian took from his finger a gorgeous carbuncle, and offered it to the eunuch. The worthy dependent of the Seraglio had a great taste in jewellery. He examined the stone with admiration, and placed it on his finger with complacency. "I require no inducements to promote the interests of science, and the purposes of charity," said the eunuch, with a patronising air. "'Tis assuredly a pretty stone, and, as the memorial of an ingenious stranger, whom I respect, I shall, with pleasure, retain it. You were saying something about a talisman. Are you serious? I doubt not that there are means which might obtain you the desired trial; but the Prince Mahomed is as violent when displeased or disappointed as munificent when gratified. Cure this Christian captive, and we may certainly receive the promised purses: fail, and your head will as assuredly be flung into the Seraglio moat, to say nothing of my own."

"Most noble sir!" said the physician, "I am willing to undertake the experiment on the terms you mention. Rest assured that the patient, if alive, must, with this remedy, speedily recover. You marvel! Believe me, had you witnessed the cures which it has already effected, you would only wonder at its otherwise incredible influence."

"You have the advantage," replied the eunuch, "of addressing a man who has seen something of the world. I travel every year to Anatolia with the Prince Mahomed. Were I a narrow-minded bigot, and had never been five miles from Adrianople in the whole course of my life, I might indeed be sceptical. But I am a patron of science, and have heard of talismans. How much might this ring weigh, think you?"

"I have heard it spoken of as a carbuncle of uncommon size," replied the Armenian.

"Where did you say you lodged, Hakim?"

"At the Khan of Bedreddin."

"A very proper dwelling. Well, we shall see. Have you more jewels? I might, perhaps, put you in the way of parting with some at good prices. The Khan of Bedreddin is very conveniently situated. I may, perhaps, towards evening, taste your coffee at the Khan of Bedreddin, and we will talk of this said talisman. Allah be with you, worthy Hakim!" The eunuch nodded, not without encouragement, and went his way.

"Anxiety alone enabled me to keep my countenance," said Nicæus. "A patron of science, forsooth! Of all the insolent, shallow-brained, rapacious coxcombs— "

"Hush, my friend!" said Iskander, with a smile. "The chief eunuch of the heir apparent of the Turkish empire is a far greater man than a poor prince, or a proscribed rebel. This worthy can do our business, and I trust will. He clearly bites, and a richer bait will, perhaps, secure him. In the meantime, we must be patient, and remember whose destiny is at stake."

CHAPTER 10

The chief eunuch did not keep the adventurous companions long in suspense; for, before the muezzin had announced the close of day from the minarets, he had reached the Khan of Bedreddin, and inquired for the Armenian physician.

"We have no time to lose," said the eunuch to Iskander. "Bring with you whatever you may require, and follow me."

The eunuch led the way, Iskander and Nicæus maintaining a respectful distance. After proceeding down several streets, they arrived at the burial-ground, where they had conversed in the morning; and when they had entered that more retired spot, the eunuch fell back, and addressed his companion.

"Now, worthy Hakim," he said, "if you deceive me, I will never patronize a man of science again. I found an opportunity of speaking to the Prince this afternoon of your talisman, and he has taken from my representations such a fancy for its immediate proof, that I found it quite impossible to postpone its trial even until to-morrow. I mentioned the terms. I told the Prince your life was the pledge. I said nothing of the moiety of the reward, worthy Hakim. That is an affair between ourselves. I trust to your honour, and I always act thus with men of science."

"I shall not disgrace my profession or your confidence, rest assured," replied Iskander. "And am I to see the captive to-night?"

"I doubt it not. Are you prepared? We might, perhaps, gain a little time, if very necessary."

"By no means, sir; Truth is ever prepared."

Thus conversing, they passed through the burial-ground, and approached some high, broad walls, forming a terrace, and planted with young sycamore-trees. The eunuch tapped with his silver stick, at a small gate, which opened, and admitted them into a garden, full of large clumps of massy shrubs. Through these a winding walk led for some way, and then conducted them to an open lawn, on which was situate a vast and irregular building. As they approached the pile, a young man of very imperious aspect rushed forward from a gate, and abruptly accosted Iskander.

"Are you the Armenian physician?" he inquired.

Iskander bowed assent.

"Have you got your talisman? You know the terms? Cure this Christian girl and you shall name your own reward; fail, and I shall claim your forfeit head."

"The terms are well understood, mighty Prince," said Iskander, for the young man was no less a personage than the son of Amurath, and future conqueror of Constantinople; "but I am confident there will be no necessity for the terror of Christendom claiming any other heads than those of his enemies."

"Kaflis will conduct you at once to your patient," said Mahomed. "For myself, I cannot rest until I know the result of your visit. I shall wander about these gardens, and destroy the flowers, which is the only pleasure now left me."

Kaflis motioned to his companions to advance, and they entered the Seraglio.

At the end of a long gallery they came to a great portal, which Kaflis opened, and Iskander and Nicæus for a moment supposed that they had arrived at the chief hall of the Tower of Babel, but they found the shrill din only proceeded from a large company of women, who were employed in distilling the rare atar of the jasmine flower. All their voices ceased on the entrance of the strangers, as if by a miracle; but when they had examined them, and observed that it was only a physician and his boy, their awe, or their surprise, disappeared; and they crowded round Iskander, some holding out their wrists, others lolling out their tongues, and some asking questions, which perplexed alike the skill and the modesty of the adventurous dealer in magical medicine. The annoyance, however, was not of great duration, for Kaflis so belaboured their fair shoulders with his official baton, that they instantly retreated with precipitation, uttering the most violent shrieks, and bestowing on the eunuch so many titles, that Iskander and his page were quite astounded at the intuitive knowledge which the imprisoned damsels possessed of that vocabulary of abuse, which is in general mastered only by the experience of active existence.

Quitting this chamber, the eunuch and his companions ascended a lofty staircase. They halted at length before a door. "This is the chamber of the tower," said their guide, "and here we shall find the fair captive." He knocked, the door was opened by a female slave, and Iskander and Nicæus, with an anxiety they could with difficulty conceal, were ushered into a small but sumptuous apartment. In the extremity was a recess covered with a light gauzy curtain. The eunuch bidding them keep in the background, advanced, and cautiously withdrawing the curtain slightly aside, addressed some words in a low voice to the inmate of the recess. In a few minutes the eunuch beckoned to Iskander to advance, and whispered to him: "She would not at first see you, but I have told her you are a Christian, the more the pity, and she consents." So saying, he withdrew the curtain, and exhibited a veiled female figure lying on a couch.

"Noble lady," said the physician in Greek, which he had ascertained the eunuch did not comprehend; "pardon the zeal of a Christian friend. Though habited in this garb, I have served under your illustrious sire. I should deem my life well spent in serving the daughter of the great Hunniades."

"Kind stranger," replied the captive, "I was ill prepared for such a meeting. I thank you for your sympathy, but my sad fortunes are beyond human aid."

"God works by humble instruments, noble lady," said Iskander, "and with his blessing we may yet prosper."

"I fear that I must look to death as my only refuge," replied Iduna, "and still more, I fear that it is not so present a refuge as my oppressors themselves imagine. But you are a physician; tell me then how speedily Nature will make me free."

She held forth her hand, which Iskander took and involuntarily pressed. "Noble lady," he said, "my skill is a mere pretence to enter these walls. The only talisman I bear with me is a message from your friends."

"Indeed!" said Iduna, in an agitated tone.

"Restrain yourself, noble lady," said Iskander, interposing, "restrain yourself. Were you any other but the daughter of Hunniades I would not have ventured upon this perilous exploit. But I know that the Lady Iduna has inherited something more than the name of her great ancestors—their heroic soul. If ever there were a moment in her life in which it behoved her to exert all her energies, that moment has arrived. The physician who addresses her, and his attendant who waits at hand, are two of the Lady Iduna's most devoted friends. There is nothing that they will not hazard, to effect her delivery; and they have matured a plan of escape which they are sanguine must succeed. Yet its completion will require, on her part, great anxiety of mind, greater exertion of body, danger, fatigue, privation. Is the Lady Iduna prepared for all this endurance, and all this hazard?"

"Noble friend," replied Iduna, "for I cannot deem you a stranger, and none but a most chivalric knight could have entered upon this almost forlorn adventure; you have not, I trust, miscalculated my character. I am a slave, and unless heaven will interpose, must soon be a dishonoured one. My freedom and my fame are alike at stake. There is no danger, and no suffering which I will not gladly welcome, provided there be even a remote chance of regaining my liberty and securing my honour."

"You are in the mind I counted on. Now, mark my words, dear lady. Seize an opportunity this evening of expressing to your gaolers that you have already experienced some benefit from my visit, and announce your rising confidence in my skill. In the meantime I will make such a report that our daily meetings will not be difficult. For the present, farewell. The Prince Mahomed waits without, and I would exchange some words with him before I go."

"And must we part without my being acquainted with the generous friends to whom I am indebted for an act of devotion which almost reconciles me to my sad fate?" said Iduna. "You will not, perhaps, deem the implicit trust reposed in you by one whom you have no interest to deceive, and who, if deceived, cannot be placed in a worse position than she at present fills, as a very gratifying mark of confidence, yet that trust is reposed in you; and let me, at least, soothe the galling dreariness of my solitary hours, by the recollection of the friends to whom I am indebted for a deed of friendship which has filled me with a feeling of wonder from which I have not yet recovered."

"The person who has penetrated the Seraglio of Constantinople in disguise to rescue the Lady Iduna," answered Iskander, "is the Prince Nicæus."

"Nicæus!" exclaimed Iduna, in an agitated tone. "The voice to which I listen is surely not that of the Prince Nicæus; nor the form on which I gaze," she added, as she unveiled. Beside her stood the tall figure of the Armenian physician. She beheld his swarthy and unrecognised countenance. She cast her dark eyes around with an air of beautiful perplexity.

"I am a friend of the Prince Nicæus," said the physician. "He is here. Shall he advance? Alexis," called cut, Iskander, not waiting for her reply. The page of the physician came forward, but the eunuch accompanied him. "All is right," said Iskander to Kaflis. "We are sure of our hundred purses. But, without doubt, with any other aid, the case were desperate."

"There is but one God," said the eunuch, polishing his carbuncle, with a visage radiant as the gem. "I never repented patronizing men of science. The prince waits without. Come along!" He took Iskander by the arm. "Where is your boy? What are you doing there, sir?" inquired the eunuch, sharply, of Nicæus, who, was tarrying behind, and kissing the hand of Iduna.

"I was asking the lady for a favour to go to the coffee-house with;" replied Nicæus, "you forget that I am to have none of the hundred purses."

"True," said the eunuch; "there is something in that. Here, boy, here is a piastre for you. I like to encourage men of science, and all that belong to them. Do not go and spend it all in one morning, boy, and when the fair captive is cured, if you remind me, boy, perhaps I may give you another."

CHAPTER 11

Kaflis and his charge again reached the garden. The twilight was nearly past. A horseman galloped up to them, followed by several running footmen. It was the prince.

"Well, Hakim," he inquired, in his usual abrupt style, "can you cure her?"

"Yes;" answered Iskander, firmly.

"Now listen, Hakim," said Mahomed. "I must very shortly leave the city, and proceed into Epirus at the head of our troops. I have sworn two things, and I have sworn them by the holy stone. Ere the new moon, I will have the heart of Iduna and the head of Iskander!"

The physician bowed.

"If you can so restore the health of this Frangy girl," continued Mahomed, "that she may attend me within ten days into Epirus, you shall claim from my treasury what sum you like, and become physician to the Seraglio. What say you?"

"My hope and my belief is," replied Iskander, "that within ten days she may breathe the air of Epirus."

"By my father's beard, you are a man after my own heart," exclaimed the prince; "and since thou dealest in talismans, Hakim, can you give me a charm that you will secure me a meeting with this Epirot rebel within the term, so that I may keep my oath. What say you? what say you?"

"There are such spells," replied Iskander. "But mark, I can only secure the meeting, not the head."

"That is my part," said Mahomed, with an arrogant sneer. "But the meeting, the meeting?"

"You know the fountain of Kallista in Epirus. Its virtues are renowned."

"I have beard of it."

"Plunge your scimitar in its midnight waters thrice, on the eve of the new moon, and each time summon the enemy you would desire to meet. He will not fail you."

"If you cure the captive, I will credit the legend, and keep the appointment," replied Mahomed, thoughtfully.

"I have engaged to do that," replied the physician.

"Well, then, I shall redeem my pledge," said the prince

"But mind," said the physician, "while I engage to cure the lady and produce the warrior, I can secure your highness neither the heart of the one nor the head of the other."

"'Tis understood," said Mahomed.

CHAPTER 12

The Armenian physician did not fail to attend his captive patient at an early hour on the ensuing morn. His patron Kaflis received him with an encouraging smile.

"The talisman already works;" said the eunuch: "she has passed a good night, and confesses to an improvement. Our purses are safe. Methinks I already count the gold. But I say, worthy Hakim, come hither, come hither," and Kaflis looked around to be sure that no one was within hearing, "I say," and here he put on a very mysterious air indeed, "the prince is generous; you understand? We go shares. We shall not quarrel. I never yet repented patronizing a man of science, and I am sure I never shall. The prince, you see, is violent, but generous. I would not cure her too soon, eh?"

"You take a most discreet view of affairs," responded Iskander, with an air of complete assent, and they entered the chamber of the tower.

Iduna performed her part with great dexterity; but, indeed, it required less skill than herself and her advisers had at first imagined. Her malady, although it might have ended fatally, was in its origin entirely mental, and the sudden prospect of freedom, and of restoration to her country and her family, at a moment when she had delivered herself up to despair, afforded her a great and instantaneous benefit. She could not, indeed, sufficiently restrain her spirits, and smiled incredulously when Iskander mentioned the impending exertion and fatigues with doubt and apprehension. His anxiety to return immediately to Epirus, determined him to adopt the measures for her rescue without loss of time, and on his third visit, he prepared her for making the great attempt on the ensuing morn. Hitherto Iskander had refrained from revealing himself to Iduna. He was induced to adopt this conduct by various considerations. He could no longer conceal from himself that the daughter of Hunniades exercised an influence over his feelings which he was unwilling to encourage. His sincere friendship for Nicæus, and his conviction that It was his present duty to concentrate all his thought and affection in the cause of his country, would have rendered him anxious to have resisted any emotions of the kind, even could he have flattered himself that there was any chance of their being returned by the object of his rising passion. But Iskander was as modest as he was brave and gifted. The disparity of age between himself and Iduna appeared an insuperable barrier to his hopes, even had there been no other obstacle. Iskander struggled with his love, and with his strong mind the struggle, though painful, was not without success. He felt that he was acting in a manner which must ultimately tend to the advantage of his country, the happiness of his friend, and perhaps the maintenance of his own self-respect. For he had too much pride not to be very sensible to the bitterness of rejection.

Had he perceived more indications of a very cordial feeling subsisting between Nicæus and Iduna, he would perhaps not have persisted in maintaining his disguise. But he had long suspected that the passion of the Prince of Athens was not too favourably considered by the daughter of Hunniades, and he was therefore exceedingly anxious that Nicæus should possess all the credit of the present adventure, which Iskander scarcely doubted, if successful, would allow Nicæus to urge irresistible claims to the heart of a mistress whom he had rescued at the peril of his life from slavery and dishonour, to offer rank, reputation, and love. Iskander took, therefore, several opportunities of leading Iduna to believe that he was merely the confidential agent of Nicæus, and that the whole plan of her rescue from the Seraglio of Adrianople bad been planned by his young friend. In the meantime, during the three days on which they had for short intervals met, very few words had been interchanged between Nicæus and his mistress. Those words, indeed, had been to him of the most inspiring nature, and expressed such a deep scale of gratitude, and such lively regard, that Nicæus could no longer resist the delightful conviction that he had at length created a permanent interest in her heart. Often he longed to rush to her couch, and press her hand to his lips. Even the anticipation of future happiness could not prevent him from envying the good fortune of Iskander, who was allowed to converse with her without restraint; and bitterly, on their return to the khan, did he execrate the pompous eunuch for all the torture which he occasioned him by his silly conversation, and the petty tyranny of office with which Kaflis always repressed his attempts to converse for a moment with Iduna.

In the meantime all Adrianople sounded with the preparations for the immediate invasion of Epirus, and the return of Iskander to his country became each hour more urgent. Everything being prepared, the adventurers determined on the fourth morning to attempt the rescue. They repaired as usual to the Serail, and were attended by Kaflis to the chamber of the tower, who congratulated Iskander on their way on the rapid convalescence of the captive. When they had fairly entered the chamber, the physician being somewhat in advance, Nicæus, who was behind, commenced proceedings by knocking down the eunuch, and Iskander instantly turning round to his assistance, they succeeded in gagging and binding the alarmed and astonished Kaflis. Iduna then exhibited herself in a costume exactly similar to that worn by Nicæus, and which her friends had brought to her in their big. Iskander and Iduna then immediately quitted the Serail without notice or suspicion, and hurried to the khan, where they mounted their horses, that were in readiness, and hastened without a moment's loss of time to a fountain without the gates, where they awaited the arrival of Nicæus with anxiety. After remaining a few minutes in the chamber of the tower, the Prince of Athens stole out, taking care to secure the door upon Kaflis, he descended the staircase, and escaped through the Serail without meeting any one, and had nearly reached the gate of the gardens, when he was challenged by some of the eunuch guard at a little distance.

"Hilloa!" exclaimed one; "I thought you passed just now?"

"So I did," replied Nicæus, with nervous effrontery; "but I came back for my bag, which I left behind," and, giving them no time to reflect, he pushed his way through the gate with all the impudence of a page. He rushed through the burial-ground, hurried through the streets, mounted his horse, and galloped through the gates. Iskander and Iduna were in sight, he waved his hand for them at once to proceed, and in a moment, without exchanging a word, they were all galloping at full speed, nor did they breathe their horses until sunset.

By nightfall they had reached a small wood of chestnut-trees, where they rested for two hours, more for the sake of their steeds than their own refreshment, for anxiety prevented Iduna from indulging in any repose, as much as excitement prevented her from feeling any fatigue. Iskander lit a fire and prepared their rough meal, unharnessed the horses, and turned them out to their pasture. Nicæus made Iduna a couch of fern and supported her head, while, in deference to his entreaties she endeavoured in vain to sleep. Before midnight they were again on their way, and proceeded at a rapid pace towards the mountains, until a few hours before noon, when their horses began to sink under the united influence of their previous exertions and the increasing heat of the day. Iskander looked serious, and often threw a backward glance in the direction of Adrianople.

"We must be beyond pursuit," said Nicæus. "I dare say poor Kaflis is still gagged and bound."

"Could we but reach the mountains," replied his companion, "I should have little fear, but I counted upon our steeds carrying us there without faltering. We cannot reckon upon more than three hours' start, prince. Our friend Kaflis is too important a personage to be long missed."

"The Holy Virgin befriend us!" said the Lady Iduna. "I ca urge my poor horse no more."

They had now ascended a small rising ground, which gave the wide prospect over the plain. Iskander halted and threw an anxious glance around him.

"There are some horsemen in the distance whom I do not like," said the physician.

"I see them," said Nicæus; "travellers like ourselves."

"Let us die sooner than be taken," said Iduna.

"Move on," said the physician, "and let me observe these horsemen alone. I would there were some forest at hand. In two hours we may gain the mountains."

The daughter of Hunniades and the Prince of Athens descended the rising ground. Before them, but at a considerable distance was a broad and rapid river, crossed by a ruinous Roman bridge. The opposite bank of the river was the termination of a narrow plain, which led immediately to the mountains.

"Fair Iduna, you are safe," said the Prince of Athens.

"Dear Nicæus," replied his companion, "imagine what I feel."

"It is too wild a moment to express my gratitude."

"I trust that Iduna will never express her gratitude to Nicæus," answered the prince; "it is not, I assure you, a favourite word with him."

Their companion rejoined them, urging his wearied horse to its utmost speed.

"Nicæus!" he called out, "halt."

They stopped their willing horses.

"How now! my friend;" said the prince; "you look grave."

"Lady Iduna!" said the Armenian, "we are pursued."

Hitherto the prospect of success, and the consciousness of the terrible destiny that awaited failure, had supported Iduna under exertions, which under any other circumstances must have proved fatal. But to learn, at the very moment that she was congratulating herself on the felicitous completion of their daring enterprise, that that dreaded failure was absolutely impending, demanded too great an exertion of her exhausted energies. She turned pale; she lifted up her imploring hands and eyes to heaven in speechless agony, and then, bending down her head, wept with unrestrained and harrowing violence. The distracted Nicæus sprung from his horse, endeavoured to console the almost insensible Iduna, and then woefully glancing at his fellow adventurer, wrung his hands in despair. His fellow adventurer seemed lost in thought.

"They come," said Nicæus, starting; "methinks I see one on the brow of the hill. Away! fly! Let us at least die fighting. Dear, dear Iduna, would that my life could ransom thine! O God! this is indeed agony."

"Escape is impossible," said Iduna, in a tone of calmness which astonished them. "They must overtake us. Alas! brave friends, I have brought ye to this! Pardon me, pardon me! I am ashamed of my selfish grief. Ascribe it to other causes than a narrow spirit and a weak mind. One course alone is left to us. We must not be taken prisoners. Ye are warriors, and can die as such. I am only a woman, but I am the daughter of Hunniades. Nicæus, you are my father's friend; I beseech you sheathe your dagger in my breast."

The prince in silent agony pressed his hands to his sight. His limbs quivered with terrible emotion. Suddenly he advanced and threw himself at the feet of his hitherto silent comrade. "Oh! Iskander!" exclaimed Nicæus, "great and glorious friend! my head and heart are both too weak for these awful trials; save her, save her!"

"Iskander! exclaimed the thunderstruck Iduna. Iskander!"

"I have, indeed, the misfortune to be Iskander, beloved lady," he replied. "This is, indeed, a case almost of desperation, but if I have to endure more than most men, I have, to inspire me, influences which fall to the lot of few, yourself and Epirus. Come! Nicæus, there is but one chance, we must gain the bridge." Thus speaking, Iskander caught Iduna in his arms, and remounting his steed, and followed by the Prince of Athens, hurried towards the river.

"The water is not fordable," said Iskander, when they had arrived at its bank. "The bridge I shall defend; and it will go hard if I do not keep them at bay long enough for you and Iduna to gain the mountains. Away; think no more of me; nay! no tear, dear lady, or you will unman me. An ins inspiring smile, and all will go well. Hasten to Croia, and let nothing tempt you to linger in the vicinity, with the hope of my again joining you. Believe me, we shall meet again, but act upon what I say, as if they were my dying words. God bless you, Nicæus! No murmuring. For once let the physician, indeed, command his page. Gentle lady, commend me to your father. Would I had such a daughter in Epirus, to head my trusty brethren if I fall. Tell the great Hunniades my legacy to him is my country. Farewell, farewell!"

"I will not say farewell!" exclaimed Iduna; "I too can fight. I will stay and die with you."

"See they come! Believe me I shall conquer. Fly, fly, thou noble girl! Guard her well, Nicæus. God bless thee, boy! Live and be happy. Nay, nay, not another word. The farther ye are both distant, trust me, the stronger will be my arm. Indeed, indeed, I do beseech ye, fly!"

Nicæus placed the weeping Iduna in her saddle, and after leading her horse over the narrow and broken bridge, mounted his own, and then they ascended together the hilly and winding track. Iskander watched them as they went. Often Iduna waved her kerchief to her forlorn champion. In the meantime Iskander tore off his Armenian robes and flung them into the river, tried his footing on the position he had taken up, stretched his limbs, examined his daggers, flourished his scimitar.

The bridge would only permit a single rider to pass abreast. It was supported by three arches, the centre one of very considerable size, the others small, and rising out of the shallow water on each side. In many parts the parapet wall was broken, in some even the pathway was almost impassable from the masses of fallen stone, and the dangerous fissures. In the centre of the middle arch was an immense key-stone, on which was sculptured, in high relief, an enormous helmet, which indeed gave, among the people of the country, a title to the bridge.

A band of horsemen dashed at full speed, with a loud shout, down the bill. They checked their horses, when to their astonishment they found Iskander with his drawn scimitar, prepared to resist their passage. But they paused only for a moment, and immediately attempted to swim the river. But their exhausted horses drew back with a strong instinct from the rushing waters: one of the band alone, mounted on a magnificent black mare, succeeding in his purpose. The rider was half-way in the stream, his high-bred steed snorting and struggling in the strong current. Iskander, with the same ease as if he were plucking the ripe fruit from a tree, took up a ponderous stone, and hurled it with fatal precision at his adventurous enemy. The rider shrieked and fell, and rose no more: the mare, relieved from her burthen, exerted all her failing energies, and succeeded in gaining the opposite bank. There, rolling herself in the welcome pasture, and neighing with a note of triumph, she revelled in her hard escape.

"Cut down the Giaour!" exclaimed one of the horsemen, and he dashed at the bridge. His fragile blade shivered into a thousand pieces as it crossed the scimitar of Iskander, and in a moment his bleeding head fell over the parapet.

Instantly the whole band, each emulous of revenging his comrades, rushed without thought at Iskander, and endeavoured to overpower him by their irresistible charge. His scimitar flashed like lightning. The two foremost of his enemies fell, but the impulse of the numbers prevailed, and each instant, although dealing destruction with every blow, he felt himself losing ground. At length he was on the centre of the centre arch, an eminent position, which allowed him for a moment to keep them at bay, and gave him breathing time. Suddenly he made a desperate charge, clove the head of the leader of the band in two, and beat them back several yards; then swiftly returning to his former position, he summoned all his supernatural strength, and stamping on the mighty, but mouldering keystone, he forced it from its form, and broke the masonry of a thousand years. Amid a loud and awful shriek, horses and horsemen, and the dissolving fragments of the scene for a moment mingled as it were in airy chaos, and then plunged with a horrible plash into the fatal depths below. Some fell, and, stunned by the massy fragments, rose no more; others struggled again into light, and gained with difficulty their old shore. Amid them, Iskander, unhurt, swam like a river god, and stabbed to the heart the only strong swimmer that was making his way in the direction of Epirus. Drenched and exhausted, Iskander at length stood upon the opposite margin, and wrung his garments, while he watched the scene of strange destruction.

Three or four exhausted wretches were lying bruised and breathless on the opposite bank: one drowned horse was stranded near them, caught by the rushes. Of all that brave company the rest had vanished, and the broad, and blue, and sunny waters rushed without a shadow beneath the two remaining arches.

"Iduna! thou art safe," exclaimed Iskander. "Now for Epirus!" So saying, he seized the black mare, renovated by her bath and pasture, and vaulting on her back, was in a few minutes bounding over his native hills.

CHAPTER 13

In the meantime let us not forget the Prince of Athens and the Lady Iduna. These adventurous companions soon lost sight of their devoted champion, and entered a winding ravine, which gradually brought them to the summit of the first chain of the Epirot mountains. From it they looked down upon a vast and rocky valley, through which several mule tracks led in various directions, and entered the highest barrier of the mountains, which rose before them covered with forests of chestnut and ilex. Nicæus chose the track which he considered least tempting to pursuit, and towards sunset they had again entered a ravine washed by a mountain stream. The course of the waters had made the earth fertile and beautiful. Wild shrubs of gay and pleasant colours refreshed their wearied eye-sight, and the perfume of aromatic plants invigorated their jaded senses. Upon the bank of the river, too, a large cross of roughly-carved wood brought comfort to their Christian hearts, and while the holy emblem filled them with hope and consolation, and seemed an omen of refuge from their Moslemin oppressors, a venerable Eremite, with a long white beard descending over his dark robes, and leaning on a staff of thorn, came forth from an adjoining cavern to breathe the evening air and pour forth his evening orisons.

Iduna and Nicæus had hitherto prosecuted their sorrowful journey almost in silence. Exhausted with anxiety, affliction, and bodily fatigue, with difficulty the daughter of Hunniades could preserve her seat upon her steed. One thought alone interested her, and by its engrossing influence maintained her under all her sufferings, the memory of Iskander. Since she first met him, at the extraordinary interview in her father's pavilion, often had the image of the hero recurred to her fancy, often had she mused over his great qualities and strange career. His fame, so dangerous to female hearts, was not diminished by his presence. And now, when Iduna recollected that she was indebted to him for all that she held dear, that she owed to his disinterested devotion, not only life, but all that renders life desirable, honour and freedom, country and kindred, that image was invested with associations and with sentiments, which, had Iskander himself been conscious of their existence, would have lent redoubled vigour to his arm, and fresh inspiration to his energy. More than once Iduna had been on the point of inquiring of Nicæus the reason which had induced alike him and Iskander to preserve so strictly the disguise of his companion. But a feeling which she did not choose to analyse struggled successfully with her curiosity: she felt a reluctance to speak of Iskander to the Prince of Athens. In the meantime Nicæus himself was not apparently very anxious of conversing upon the subject, and after the first rapid expressions of fear and hope as to the situation of their late comrade, they relapsed into silence, seldom broken by Nicæus, but to deplore the sufferings of his mistress, lamentations which Iduna answered with a faint smile.

The refreshing scene wherein they had now entered, and the cheering appearance of the Eremite, were subjects of mutual congratulation; and Nicæus, somewhat advancing, claimed the attention of the holy man, announcing their faith, imprisonment, escape, and sufferings, and entreating hospitality and refuge. The Eremite pointed with his staff to the winding path, which ascended the bank of the river to the cavern, and welcomed the pilgrims, in the name of their blessed Saviour, to his wild abode and simple fare.

The cavern widened when they entered, and comprised several small apartments. It was a work of the early Christians, who had found a refuge in their days of persecution, and art had completed the beneficent design of nature. The cavern was fresh, and sweet, and clean. Heaven smiled upon its pious inmate through an aperture in the roof; the floor was covered with rushes; in one niche rested a brazen cross, and in another a perpetual lamp burnt before a picture, where Madonna smiled with meek tenderness upon her young divinity.

The Eremite placed upon a block of wood, the surface of which he had himself smoothed, some honey, some dried fish and a wooden bowl filled from the pure stream that flowed beneath them: a simple meal, but welcome. His guests seated themselves upon a rushy couch, and while they refreshed themselves, he gently inquired the history of their adventures. As it was evident that the Eremite, from her apparel, mistook the sex of Iduna, Nicæus thought fit not to undeceive him, but passed her off as his brother. He described themselves as two Athenian youths, who had been captured while serving as volunteers under the great Hunniades, and who had effected their escape from Adrianople under circumstances of great peril and difficulty; and when he had gratified the Eremite's curiosity respecting their Christian brethren in Paynim lands, and sympathetically marvelled with him at the advancing fortunes of the Crescent, Nicæus, who perceived that Iduna stood in great need of rest, mentioned the fatigues of his more fragile brother, and requested permission for him to retire. Whereupon the Eremite himself, fetching a load of fresh rushes, arranged them in one of the cells, and invited the fair Iduna to repose. The daughter of Hunniades, first humbling herself before the altar of the Virgin, and offering her gratitude for all the late mercies vouchsafed unto her, and then bidding a word of peace to her host and her companion, withdrew to her hard-earned couch, soon was buried in a sleep as sweet and innocent as herself.

But repose fell not upon the eye-lids of Nicæus in spite of all labours. The heart of the Athenian Prince was distracted by two most powerful of passions—Love and Jealousy—and when the Eremite, pointing out to his guest his allotted resting-place, himself retired to his regular and simple slumbers, Nicæus quitted the cavern, and standing upon the bank of the river, gazed in abstraction upon the rushing waters foaming in the moonlight. The Prince of Athens, with many admirable qualities, was one of those men who are influenced only by their passions, and who, in the affairs of life, are invariably guided by their imagination instead of their reason. At present all thought and feeling, all considerations, and all circumstances, merged in the overpowering love he entertained for Iduna, his determination to obtain her at all cost and peril, and his resolution that she should never again meet Iskander, except as the wife of Nicæus. Compared with this paramount object, the future seemed to vanish. The emancipation of his country, the welfare of his friend, even the maintenance of his holy creed, all those great and noble objects for which, under other circumstances, he would have been prepared to sacrifice his fortune and his life, no longer interested or influenced him; and while the legions of the Crescent were on the point of pouring into Greece to crush that patriotic and Christian cause over which Iskander and himself had so often mused, whose interests the disinterested absence of Iskander, occasioned solely by his devotion to Nicæus, had certainly endangered, and perhaps, could the events of the last few hours be known, even sacrificed, the Prince of Athens resolved, unless Iduna would consent to become his, at once to carry off the daughter of Hunniades to some distant country. Nor indeed, even with his easily excited vanity, was Nicæus sanguine of obtaining his purpose by less violent means. He was already a rejected suitor, and under circumstances which scarcely had left hope. Nothing but the sole credit of her chivalric rescue could perhaps have obtained for him the interest in the heart of Iduna which he coveted. For while this exploit proffered an irresistible claim to her deepest gratitude, it indicated also, on the part of her deliverer, the presence and possession of all those great qualities, the absence of which in the character and conduct of her suitor, Iduna had not, at a former period, endeavoured to conceal to be the principal came of his rejection. And now, by the unhappy course of circumstances, the very deed on which he counted, with sanguine hope, as the sure means of his success, seemed as it were to have placed him in a more inferior situation than before. The constant society of his mistress had fanned to all its former force and ardour, the flame which, apart from her, and hopeless, he had endeavoured to repress; while, on the other hand, he could not conceal from himself, that Iduna must feel that he had played in these rest proceeding but a secondary part; that all the genius and all the generosity of the exploit rested with Iskander, who, after having obtained her freedom by so much energy, peril, sagacity and skill, had secured it by a devoted courage which might shame all the knights of Christendom; perhaps, too, had secured it by his own life.

What if Iskander were no more? It was a great contingency. The eternal servitude of Greece, and the shameful triumph of the Crescent, were involved, perhaps, in that single event. And could the possession of Iduna compensate for such disgrace and infamy? Let us not record the wild response of passion.

It was midnight ere the restless Nicæus, more exhausted by his agitating reverie than by his previous exertions, returned into the cavern, and found refuge in sleep from all his disquietudes.

CHAPTER 14

The Eremite rose with the Sun; and while he was yet at matins, was joined by Iduna, refreshed and cheerful after her unusual slumbers. After performing their devotions, her venerable host proposed that they should go forth and enjoy the morning air. So, descending the precipitous bank of the river, he led the way to a small glen, the bed of a tributary rivulet, now nearly exhausted. Beautiful clumps of birch-trees and tall thin poplars, rose on each side among the rocks covered with bright mosses, and parasitical plants of gay and various colours. One side of the glen was touched with the golden and grateful beams of the rising sun, and the other was in deep shadow.

"Here you can enjoy nature and freedom in security;" said the Eremite, "for your enemies, if they have not already given up their pursuit, will scarcely search this sweet solitude."

"It is indeed sweet, holy father," said Iduna; "but the captive, who has escaped from captivity, can alone feel all its sweetness."

"It is true," said the Eremite; "I also have been a captive."

"Indeed! holy father. To the Infidels?"

"To the Infidels, gentle pilgrim."

"Have you been at Adrianople?"

"My oppressors were not the Paynim," replied the Eremite, "but they were enemies far more dire, my own evil passions. Time was when my eye sparkled like thine, gentle pilgrim, and my heart was not as pure."

"God is merciful," said Iduna, "and without His aid, the strongest are but shadows."

"Ever think so," replied the Eremite, "and you will deserve rather His love than His mercy. Thirty long years have I spent in this solitude, meditating upon the past, and it is a theme yet fertile in instruction. My hours are never heavy, and memory is to me what action is to other men."

"You have seen much, holy father?"

"And felt more. Yet you will perhaps think the result of all my experience very slight, for I can only say unto thee, trust not in thyself."

"It is a great truth," remarked Iduna, "and leads to a higher one."

"Even so," replied the Eremite. "We are full of wisdom in old age, as in winter this river is full of water, but the fire of youth, like the summer sun, dries up the stream."

Iduna did not reply. The Eremite attracted her attention to a patch of cresses on the opposite bank of the stream. "Every morn I rise only to discover fresh instances of omnipotent benevolence," he exclaimed. "Yesterday ye tasted my honey and my fish. To-day I can offer ye a fresh dainty. We will break our fast in this pleasant glen. Rest thou here, gentle youth, and I will summon thy brother to our meal. I fear me much he does not bear so contented a spirit as thyself."

"He is older, and has seen more," replied Iduna.

The Eremite shook his head, and leaning on his staff, returned to the cavern. Iduna remained, seated on a mossy rock, listening to the awakening birds, and musing over the fate of Iskander. While she was indulging in this reverie, her name was called. She looked up with a blush, and beheld Nicæus.

"How fares my gentle comrade?" inquired the Prince of Athens.

"As well as I hope you are, dear Nicæus. We have been indeed fortunate in finding so kind a host."

"I think I may now congratulate you on your safety," said the Prince. "This unfrequented pass will lead us in two days to Epirus, nor do I indeed now fear pursuit."

"Acts and not words must express in future how much we owe to you," said Iduna. "My joy would be complete if my father only knew of our safety, and if our late companion were here to share it."

"Fear not for my friend," replied Nicæus. "I have faith in the fortune of Iskander."

"If any one could succeed under such circumstances, he doubtless is the man," rejoined Iduna; "but it was indeed an awful crisis in his fate."

"Trust me, dear lady, it is wise to banish gloomy thoughts."

"We can give him only our thoughts," said Iduna, "and when we remember how much is dependent on his life, can they be cheerful?"

"Mine must be so, when I am in the presence of Iduna," replied Nicæus.

The daughter of Hunniades gathered moss from the rock, and threw it into the stream.

"Dear lady," said the Prince of Athens, seating himself by her side, and stealing her gentle hand. "Pardon me, if an irrepressible feeling at this moment impels me to recur to a subject, which, I would fain hope, were not so unpleasing to you, as once unhappily you deemed it. O! Iduna, Iduna, best and dearest, we are once more together; once more I gaze upon that unrivalled form, and listen to the music of that matchless voice. I sought you, I perhaps violated my pledge, but I sought you in captivity and sorrow. Pardon me, pity me, Iduna! Oh! Iduna, if possible, love me!"

She turned away her head, she turned away her streaming eyes. "It is impossible not to love my deliverers," she replied, in a low and tremulous voice, "even could he not prefer the many other claims to affection which are possessed by the Prince of Athens. I was not prepared for this renewal of a most painful subject, perhaps not under any circumstances, but least of all under those in which we now find ourselves."

"Alas!" exclaimed the prince, "I can no longer control my passion. My life, not my happiness merely, depends upon Iduna becoming mine. Bear with me, my beloved, bear with me! Were you Nicæus, you too would need forgiveness."

"I beseech you, cease!" exclaimed Iduna, in a firmer voice; and, withdrawing her hand, she suddenly rose. "This is neither the time nor place for such conversation. I have not forgotten that, but a few days back, I was a hopeless captive, and that my life and fame are even now in danger. Great mercies have been vouchsafed to me; but still I perhaps need the hourly interposition of heavenly aid. Other than such worldly thoughts should fill my mind, and do. Dear Nicæus," she continued, in a more soothing tone, "you have nobly commenced a most heroic enterprise: fulfil it in like spirit."

He would have replied; but at this moment the staff of the Eremite sounded among the rocks. Baffled, and dark with rage and passion, the Prince of Athens quitted Iduna, and strolled towards the upper part of the glen, to conceal his anger and disappointment.

"Eat, gentle youth," said the Eremite. "Will not thy brother join us? What may be his name?"

"Nicæus, holy father."

"And thine?"

Iduna blushed and hesitated. At length, in her confusion, she replied, "Iskander."

"Nicæus," called out the Eremite, "Iskander and myself await thee!"

Iduna trembled. She was agreeably surprised when the prince returned with a smiling countenance, and joined in the meal, with many cheerful words.

"Now I propose," said the Eremite, "that yourself and your brother Iskander should tarry with me some days, if, indeed, my simple fare have any temptation."

"I thank thee, holy father," replied Nicæus, "but our affairs are urgent; nor indeed could I have tarried here at all, had it not been for my young Iskander here, who, as you may easily believe, is little accustomed to his late exertions. But, indeed, towards sunset, we must proceed."

"Bearing with us," added Iduna, "a most grateful recollection of our host."

"God be with ye, wherever ye may proceed," replied the Eremite.

"My trust is indeed in Him," rejoined Iduna.

CHAPTER 15

And so, two hours before sunset, mounting their refreshed horses, Nicæus and Iduna quitted, with many kind words, the cavern of the Eremite, and took their way along the winding bank of the river. Throughout the moonlit night they travelled, ascending the last and highest chain of mountains and reaching the summit by dawn. The cheerful light of morning revealed to them the happy plains of a Christian country. With joyful spirits they descended into the fertile land, and stopped at a beautiful Greek village, embowered in orchards and groves of olive-trees.

The Prince of Athens instantly inquired for the Primate, or chief personage of the village, and was conducted to his house; but its master, he was informed, was without, supervising the commencement of the vintage. Leaving Iduna with the family of the Primate, Nicæus went in search of him. The vineyard was full of groups, busied in the most elegant and joyous of human occupations, gathering, with infinite bursts of merriment, the harvest of the vine. Some mounted on ladders, fixed against the festooning branches, plucked the rich bunches, and threw them below, where girls, singing in chorus, caught them in panniers, or their extended drapery. In the centre of the vineyard, a middle-aged man watched with a calm, but vigilant eye, the whole proceedings, and occasionally stimulated the indolent, or prompted the inexperienced.

"Christo," said the Prince of Athens, when he had approached him. The Primate turned round, but evidently did not immediately recognise the person who addressed him.

"I see," continued the prince, "that my meditated caution was unnecessary. My strange garb is a sufficient disguise."

"The Prince Nicæus!" exclaimed the Primate. "He is, indeed, disguised, but will, I am sure, pardon his faithful servant."

"Not a word, Christo!" replied the prince. "To be brief, I have crossed the mountains from Roumelia, and have only within this hour recognised the spot whither I have chanced to arrive. I have a companion with me. I would not be known. You comprehend?

Affairs of state. I take it for granted that there are none here who will recognise me, after three years' absence, in this dress."

"You may feel secure, my lord," replied Christo. "If you puzzled me, who have known you since you were no bigger than this bunch of grapes, you will quite confound the rest."

"'Tis well. I shall stay here a day or two, in order to give them an opportunity to prepare for my reception. In the meantime, it is necessary to send on a courier at once. You must manage all this for me, Christo. How are your daughters?"

"So, so, please your Highness," replied Christo. "A man with seven daughters has got trouble for every day in the week."

"But not when they are so pretty as yours are!"

"Poh! poh! handsome is that handsome does; and as for Alexina, she wants to be married."

"Very natural. Let her marry, by all means."

"But Helena wants to do the same."

"More natural still; for, if possible, she is prettier. For my part, I could marry them both."

"Ay, ay! that is all very well; but handsome is that handsome does. I have no objection to Alexina marrying, and even Helena; but then there is Lais— "

"Hah! hah! hah!" exclaimed the prince. "I see, my dear Christo, that my foster sisters give you a very proper portion of trouble. However, I must be off to my travelling companion. Come in as soon as you can, my dear fellow, and will settle everything. A good vintage to you, and only as much mischief as necessary." So saying, the prince tripped away.

"Well! who would have thought of seeing him here!" exclaimed the worthy Primate. "The same gay dog as ever! What can he have been doing at Roumelia? Affairs of state, indeed! I'll wager my new Epiphany scarf, that, whatever the affairs are, there is a pretty girl in the case."

CHAPTER 16

The fair Iduna, after all her perils and sufferings, was at length sheltered in safety under a kind and domestic roof. Alexina, and Helena, and Lais, and all the other sisters emulated each other in the attentions which they lavished upon the two brothers, but especially the youngest. Their kindness, indeed, was only equalled by their ceaseless curiosity, and had they ever waited for the answers of Iduna to their questions, the daughter of Hunniades might, perhaps, have been somewhat puzzled to reconcile her responses with probability. Helena answered the questions of Alexina; Lais anticipated even Helena. All that Iduna had to do was to smile and be silent, and it was universally agreed that Iskander was singularly shy as well as excessively handsome. In the meantime, when Nicæus met Iduna in the evening of the second day of their visit, he informed her that he had been so fortunate as to resume an acquaintance with an old companion in arms in the person of a neighbouring noble, who had invited them to rest at his castle at the end of their next day's journey. He told her likewise that he had dispatched a courier to Croia to inquire after Iskander, who, he expected, in the course of a few days, would bring them intelligence to guide their future movements, and decide whether they should at once proceed to the capital of Epirus, or advance into Bulgaria, in case Hunniades was still in the field. On the morrow, therefore, they proceeded on their journey. Nicæus had procured a litter for Iduna, for which her delicate health was an excuse to Alexina and her sisters, and they were attended by a small body of well-armed cavalry, for, according to the accounts which Nicæus had received, the country was still disturbed. They departed at break of day, Nicæus riding by the side of the litter, and occasionally making the most anxious inquiries after the well-being of his fair charge. An hour after noon they rested at a well, surrounded by olive-trees, until the extreme heat was somewhat allayed; and then remounting, proceeded in the direction of an undulating ridge of green hills, that partially intersected the wide plain. Towards sunset the Prince of Athens withdrew the curtains of the litter, and called the attention of Iduna to a very fair castle, rising on a fertile eminence and sparkling in the quivering beams of dying light.

"I fear," said Nicæus, "that my friend Justinian will scarcely have returned, but we are old comrades, and he desired me to act as his Seneschal. For your sake I am sorry, Iduna, for I feel convinced that he would please you."

"It is, indeed, a fair castle," replied Iduna, "and none but a true knight deserves such a noble residence."

While she spoke the commander of the escort sounded his bugle, and they commenced the ascent of the steep, a winding road, cut through a thick wood of ever-green shrubs. The gradual and easy ascent soon brought them to a portal flanked with towers, which admitted them into the outworks of the fortification. Here they found several soldiers on guard, and the commander again sounding his bugle, the gates of the castle opened, and the Seneschal, attended by a suite of many domestics, advanced and welcomed Nicæus and Iduna. The Prince of Athens dismounting, assisted his fair companion from the litter, and leading her by the band, and preceded by the Seneschal, entered the castle.

They passed through a magnificent hall, hung with choice armour, and ascending a staircase, of Pentelic marble, were ushered into a suite of lofty chambers, lined with Oriental tapestry, and furnished with many costly couches and cabinets. While they admired a spectacle so different to anything they had recently beheld or experienced, the Seneschal, followed by a number of slaves in splendid attire, advanced and offered them rare and choice refreshments, coffee and confectionery, sherbets and spiced wines. When they had partaken of this elegant cheer, Nicæus intimated to the Seneschal that the Lady Iduna might probably wish to retire, and instantly a discreet matron, followed by six most beautiful girls, each bearing a fragrant torch of cinnamon mind roses, advanced and offered to conduct the Lady Iduna to her apartments.

The matron and her company of maidens conducted the daughter of Hunniades down a long gallery, which led to a suite of the prettiest chambers in the world. The first was an antechamber, painted like a bower, but filled with the music of living birds; the second, which was much larger, was entirely covered with Venetian mirrors, and resting on a bright Persian carpet were many couches of crimson velvet, covered with a variety of sumptuous dresses; the third room was a bath, made in the semblance of a gigantic shell. Its roof was of transparent alabaster, glowing with shadowy light.

CHAPTER 17

A flourish of trumpets announced the return of the Lady Iduna and the Prince of Athens, magnificently attired, came forward with a smile, and led her, with a compliment on her resuming the dress of her sex, if not of her country, to the banquet. Iduna was not uninfluenced by that excitement which is insensibly produced by a sudden change of scene and circumstances, and especially by an unexpected transition from hardship, peril, and suffering, to luxury, security, and enjoyment. Their spirits were elevated and gay: she smiled upon Nicæus with a cheerful sympathy. They feasted, they listened to sweet music, they talked over their late adventures, and, animated by their own enjoyment, they became more sanguine as to the fate of Iskander.

"In two or three days we shall know more," said Nicæus. "In the meantime, rest is absolutely necessary to you. It is only now that you will begin to be sensible of the exertion you have made. If Iskander be at Croia, he has already informed your father of your escape; if he have not arrived, I have arranged that a courier shall be dispatched to Hunniades from that city. Do not be anxious. Try to be happy. I am myself sanguine that you will find all well. Come, pledge me your father's health, fair lady, in this goblet of Tenedos!"

"How know I that at this moment he may not be at the point of death," replied Iduna. "When I am absent from those I love, I dream only of their unhappiness."

"At this moment also," rejoined Nicæus, "he dreams perhaps of your imprisonment among barbarians. Yet how mistaken! Let that consideration support you. Come! here is to the Eremite."

"As willing, if not as sumptuous, a host as our present one," said Iduna; "and when, by-the-bye, do you think that your friend, the Lord Justinian, will arrive?"

"Oh! never mind him," said Nicæus. "He would have arrived tomorrow, but the great news which I gave him has probably changed his plans. I told him of the approaching invasion, and he has perhaps found it necessary to visit the neighbouring chieftains, or even to go on to Croia."

"Well-a-day!" exclaimed Iduna, "I would we were in my father's camp!"

"We shall soon be there, dear lady," replied the Prince. "Come, worthy Seneschal," he added, turning to that functionary, "drink to this noble lady's happy meeting with her friends."

CHAPTER 18

Three or four days passed away at the castle of Justinian, in which Nicæus used his utmost exertions to divert the anxiety of Iduna. One day was spent in examining the castle, on another he amused her with a hawking party, on a third he carried her to the neighbouring ruins of a temple, and read his favourite Æschylus to her amid its lone and elegant columns. It was impossible for any one to be more amiable and entertaining, and Iduna could not resist recognising his many virtues and accomplishments. The courier had not yet returned from Croia, which Nicæus accounted for by many satisfactory reasons. The suspense, however, at length became so painful to Iduna, that she proposed to the Prince of Athens that they should, without further delay, proceed to that city. As usual, Nicæus was not wanting in many plausible arguments in favour of their remaining at the castle, but Iduna was resolute.

"Indeed, dear Nicæus," she said, "my anxiety to see my father, or hear from him, is so great, that there is scarcely any danger which I would not encounter to gratify my wish. I feel that I have already taxed your endurance too much. But we are no longer in a hostile land, and guards and guides are to be engaged. Let me then depart alone!"

"Iduna!" exclaimed Nicæus, reproachfully. "Alas! Iduna, you are cruel, but I did not expect this!"

"Dear Nicæus!" she answered, "you always misinterpret me! It would infinitely delight me to be restored to Hunniades by yourself, but these are no common times, and you are no common person. You forget that there is one that has greater claims upon you even than a forlorn maiden, your country. And whether Iskander be at Croia or not, Greece requires the presence and exertions of the Prince of Athens."

"I have no country," replied Nicæus, mournfully, "and no object for which to exert myself."

"Nicæus! Is this the poetic patriot who was yesterday envying Themistocles?"

"Alas! Iduna, yesterday you were my muse. I do not wonder you are wearied of this castle!" continued the prince in a melancholy tone. "This spot contains nothing to interest you; but for me, it holds all that is dear, and, O! gentle maiden, one smile from you, one smile of inspiration, and I would not envy Themistocles, and might perhaps rival him."

They were walking together in the hall of the castle; Iduna stepped aside and affected to examine a curious buckler, Nicæus followed her, and placing his arm gently in hers, led her away.

"Dearest Iduna," he said, "pardon me, but men struggle for their fate. Mine is in your power. It is a contest between misery and happiness, glory and perhaps infamy. Do not then wonder that I will not yield my chance of the brighter fortune without an effort. Once more I appeal to your pity, if not to your love. Were Iduna mine, were she to hold out but the possibility of her being mine, there is no career, solemnly I avow what solemnly I feel, there is no career of which I could not be capable, and no condition to which I would not willingly subscribe. But this certainty, or this contingency, I must have: I cannot exist without the alternative. And now upon my knees, I implore her to grant it to me!"

"Nicæus," said Iduna, "this continued recurrence to a forbidden subject is most ungenerous."

"Alas! Iduna, my life depends upon a word, which you will not speak, and you talk of generosity. No! Iduna, it is not I that I am ungenerous."

"Let me say then unreasonable, Prince Nicæus."

"Say what you like, Iduna, provided you say that you are mine."

"Pardon me, sir, I am free."

"Free! You have ever underrated me, Iduna. To whom do you owe this boasted freedom?"

"This is not the first time," remarked Iduna, "that you have reminded me of an obligation, the memory of which is indelibly impressed upon my heart, and for which even the present conversation cannot make me feel less grateful. I can never forget that I owe all that is dear to yourself and your companion."

"My companion!" replied the Prince of Athens, pale and passionate. "My companion! Am I ever to be reminded of my companion?"

"Nicæus!" said Iduna; "if you forget what is due to me, at least endeavour to remember what is due to yourself?"

"Beautiful being!" said the prince, advancing and passionately seizing her hand; "pardon me! pardon me! I am not master of my reason; I am nothing, I am nothing while Iduna hesitates!"

"She does not hesitate, Nicæus. I desire, I require, that this conversation shall cease; shall never, never be renewed."

"And I tell thee, haughty woman," said the Prince of Athens, grinding his teeth, and speaking with violent action, "that I will no longer be despised with impunity. Iduna is mine, or is no one else's."

"Is it possible?" exclaimed the daughter of Hunniades. "Is it, indeed, come to this? But why am I surprised! I have long known Nicæus. I quit this castle instantly."

"You are a prisoner," replied the prince very calmly, and leaning with folded arms against the wall.

"A prisoner!" exclaimed Iduna, a little alarmed. "A prisoner! I defy you, sir. You are only a guest like myself. I will appeal to the Seneschal in the absence of his lord. He will never permit the honour of his master's flag to be violated by the irrational caprice of a passionate boy."

"What lord?" inquired Nicæus.

"Your friend, the Lord Justinian," answered Iduna. "He could little anticipate such an abuse of his hospitality."

"My friend, the Lord Justinian!" replied Nicæus, with a malignant smile. "I am surprised that a personage of the Lady Iduna's deep discrimination should so easily be deceived by 'a passionate boy!' Is it possible that you could have supposed for a moment that there was any other lord of this castle, save your devoted slave?"

"What!" exclaimed Iduna, really frightened.

"I have, indeed, the honour of finding the Lady Iduna my guest," continued Nicæus, in a tone of bitter raillery. "This castle of Kallista, the fairest in all Epirus, I inherit from my mother. Of late I have seldom visited it; but, indeed, it will become a favourite residence of mine, if it be, as I anticipate, the scene of my nuptial ceremony."

Iduna looked around her with astonishment, then threw herself upon a couch, and burst into tears. The Prince of Athens walked up and down the hall with an air of determined coolness.

"Perfidious!" exclaimed Iduna between her sobs.

"Lady Iduna," said the prince; and he seated himself by her side. "I will not attempt to palliate a deception which your charms could alone inspire and can alone justify. Hear me, Lady Iduna, hear me with calmness. I love you; I love you with a passion which has been as constant as it is strong. My birth, my rank, my fortunes, do not disqualify me for an union with the daughter of the great Hunniades. If my personal claims may sink in comparison with her surpassing excellence, I am yet to learn that any other prince in Christendom can urge a more effective plea. I am young; the ladies of the court have called me handsome; by your great father's side I have broken some lances in your honour; and even Iduna once confessed she thought me clever. Come, come, be merciful! Let my beautiful Athens receive a fitting mistress! A holy father is in readiness dear maiden. Come now, one smile! In a few days we shall reach your father's camp, and then we will kneel, as I do now, and beg a blessing on our happy union." As he spoke, he dropped upon his knee, and stealing her hand, looked into her face. It was sorrowful and gloomy.

"It is in vain, Nicæus," said Iduna, "to appeal to your generosity; it is useless to talk of the past; it is idle to reproach you for the present. I am a woman, alone and persecuted, where I could least anticipate persecution. Nicæus, I never can be yours; and now I deliver myself to the mercy of Almighty God."

"'Tis well," said Nicæus. "From the tower of the castle you may behold the waves of the Ionian Sea. You will remain here a close prisoner, until one of my galleys arrive from Piræus to bear us to Italy. Mine you must be, Iduna. It remains for you to decide under what circumstances. Continue in your obstinacy, and you may bid farewell for ever to your country and to your father. Be reasonable, and a destiny awaits you, which offers everything that has hitherto been considered the source or cause of happiness." Thus speaking, the prince retired, leaving the Lady Iduna to her own unhappy thoughts.

CHAPTER 19

The Lady Iduna was at first inclined to view the conduct of the Prince of Athens as one of those passionate and passing ebullitions in which her long acquaintance with him had taught her he was accustomed to indulge. But when on retiring soon after to her apartments, she was informed by her attendant matron that she must in future consider herself a prisoner, and not venture again to quit them without permission, she began to tremble at the possible violence of an ill-regulated mind. She endeavoured to interest her attendant in her behalf; but the matron was too well schooled to evince any feeling or express any opinion on the subject; and indeed, at length, fairly informed Iduna that she was commanded to confine her conversation to the duties of her office.

The Lady Iduna was very unhappy. She thought of her father, she thought of Iskander. The past seemed a dream; she was often tempted to believe that she was still, and had ever been, a prisoner in the Serail of Adrianople; and that all the late wonderful incidents of her life were but the shifting scenes of some wild slumber. And then some slight incident, the sound of a bell or the sign of some holy emblem, assured her she was in a Christian land, and convinced her of the strange truth that she was indeed in captivity, and a prisoner, above all others, to the fond companion of her youth. Her indignation at the conduct of Nicæus roused her courage; she resolved to make an effort to escape. Her rooms were only lighted from above; she determined to steal forth at night into the gallery; the door was secured. She hastened back to her chamber in fear and sorrow, and wept.

Twice in the course of the day the stern and silent matron visited Iduna with her food; and as she retired, secured the door. This was the only individual that the imprisoned lady ever beheld. And thus heavily rolled on upwards of a week. On the eve of the ninth day, Iduna was surprised by the matron presenting her a letter as she quitted the chamber for the night. Iduna seized it with a feeling of curiosity not unmixed with pleasure. It was the only incident that had occurred during her captivity. She recognised the hand-writing of Nicæus, and threw it down with; vexation at her silliness in supposing, for a moment, that the matron could have been the emissary of any other person.

Yet the letter must be read, and at length she opened it. It informed her that a ship had arrived from Athens at the coast, and that to-morrow she must depart for Italy. It told her also, that the Turks, under Mahomed, had invaded Albania; and that the Hungarians, under the command of her father, had come to support the Cross. It said nothing of Iskander. But it reminded her that little more than the same time that would carry her to the coast to embark for a foreign land, would, were she wise, alike enable Nicæus to place her in her father's arms, and allow him to join in the great struggle for his country and his creed. The letter was written with firmness, but tenderly. It left, however, on the mind of Iduna an impression of the desperate resolution of the writer.

Now it so happened, that as this unhappy lady jumped from her couch, and paced the room in the perturbation of her mind, the wind of her drapery extinguished her lamp. As her attendant, or visitor, had paid her last visit for the day, there seemed little chance of its being again illumined. The miserable are always more unhappy in the dark. Light is the greatest of comforters. And so this little misfortune seemed to the forlorn Iduna almost overwhelming. And as she attempted to look around, and wrung her hands in very woe, her attention was attracted by a brilliant streak of light upon the wall, which greatly surprised her. She groped her way in its direction, and slowly stretching forth her hand, observed that it made its way through a chink in the frame of one of the great mirrors which were inlaid in the wall. And as she pressed the frame, she felt to her surprise that it sprang forward. Had she not been very cautious the advancing mirror would have struck her with great force, but she had presence of mind to withdraw her hand very gradually, repressing the swiftness of the spring. The aperture occasioned by the opening of the mirror consisted of a recess, formed by a closed-up window. An old wooden shutter, or blind, in so ruinous a state, that the light freely made its way, was the only barrier against the elements. Iduna, seizing the handle which remained, at once drew it open with little difficulty.

The captive gazed with gladdened feelings upon the free and beautiful scene. Beneath her rose the rich and aromatic shrubs tinged with the soft and silver light of eve: before her extended wide and fertile champaign, skirted by the dark and undulating mountains: in the clear sky, glittering and sharp, sparkled the first crescent of the new moon, an auspicious omen to the Moslemin invaders.

Iduna gazed with, joy upon the landscape, and then hastily descending from the recess, she placed her hands to her eyes, so long unaccustomed to the light. Perhaps, too, she indulged in momentary meditation. For suddenly seizing a number of shawls; which were lying on one of the couches, she knotted them together, and then striving with all her force, she placed the heaviest, coach on one end of the costly cord, and then throwing the other out of the window, and entrusting herself to the merciful care of the holy Virgin, the brave daughter of Hunniades successfully dropped down into the garden below.

She stopped to breathe, and to revel in her emancipated existence. It was a bold enterprise gallantly achieved. But the danger had now only commenced. She found that she had alighted at the back of the castle. She stole along upon tip-toe, timid as a fawn. She remembered a small wicket-gate that led into the open country. She arrived at the gate. It was of course guarded. The single sentinel was kneeling before an image of St. George, beside him was an empty drinking-cup and an exhausted wineskin.

"Holy Saint!" exclaimed the pious sentinel, "preserve us from all Turkish infidels!" Iduna stole behind him. "Shall men who drink no wine conquer true Christians!" continued the sentinel. Iduna placed her hand upon the lock. "We thank thee for our good vintage," said the sentinel. Iduna opened the gate with the noiseless touch which a feminine finger can alone command. "And for the rise of the Lord Iskander!" added the sentinel. Iduna escaped!

Now she indeed was free. Swiftly she ran over the wide plain. She hoped to reach some town or village before her escape could be discovered, and she hurried on for three hours without resting. She came to a beautiful grove of olive-trees that spread in extensive ramifications about the plain. And through this beautiful grove of olive-trees her path seemed to lead. So she entered and advanced. And when she had journeyed for about a mile, she came to an open and very verdant piece of ground, which was, as it were, the heart of the grove. In its centre rose a fair and antique structure of white marble, shrouding from the noon-day sun the perennial flow of a very famous fountain. It was near midnight. Iduna was wearied, and she sat down upon the steps of the fountain for rest. And while she was musing over all the strange adventures of her life, she heard a rustling in the wood, and being alarmed, she rose and hid herself behind a tree.

And while she stood there, with palpitating heart, the figure of a man advanced to the fountain from an opposite direction of the grove. He went up the steps, and looked down upon the spring as if he were about to drink, but instead of doing that, he drew his scimitar, and plunged it into the water, and called out with a loud voice the name of "Iskander!" three times. Whereupon Iduna, actuated by an irresistible impulse, came forward from her hiding-place, but instantly gave a loud shriek when she beheld the Prince Mahomed!

"Oh! night of glory!" exclaimed the prince, advancing. "Do I indeed behold the fair Iduna! This is truly magic!"

"Away! away!" exclaimed the distracted Iduna, as she endeavoured to fly from him.

"He has kept his word, that cunning leech, better than I expected," said Mahomed, seizing her.

"As well as you deserve, ravisher!" exclaimed a majestic voice. A tall figure rushed forward from the wood, and dashed back the Turk.

"I am here to complete my contract, Prince Mahomed," said the stranger, drawing his sword.

"Iskander!" exclaimed the prince.

"We have met before, prince. Let us so act now that we may meet for the last time."

"Infamous, infernal traitor," exclaimed Mahomed, "dost thou, indeed, imagine that I will sully my imperial blade with the blood of my run-away slave! No I came here to secure thy punishment, but I cannot condescend to become thy punisher. Advance, guards, and seize him! Seize them both!"

Iduna flew to Iskander, who caught her in one arm, while he waved his scimitar with the other. The guards of Mahomed poured forth from the side of the grove whence the prince had issued.

"And dost thou indeed think, Mahomed," said Iskander, "that I have been educated in the Seraglio to be duped by Moslemin craft. I offer thee single combat if thou desirest it, but combat as we may, the struggle shall be equal." He whistled, and instantly a body of Hungarians, headed by Hunniades himself, advanced from the side of the grove whence Iskander had issued.

"Come on, then," said Mahomed; "each to his man." Their swords clashed, but the principal attendants of the son of Amurath deeming the affair under the present circumstances assumed the character of a mere rash adventure, bore away the Turkish prince.

"To-morrow then, this fray shall be decided on the plains of Kallista," said Mahomed.

"Epirus is prepared," replied Iskander.

The Turks withdrew. Iskander bore the senseless form of Iduna to her father. Hunniades embraced his long-lost child. They sprinkled her face with water from the fountain. She revived.

"Where is Nicæus?" inquired Iskander; "and how came you again, dear lady, in the power of Mahomed?"

"Alas! noble sir, my twice deliverer," answered Iduna, "I have, indeed, again been doomed to captivity, but my persecutor, I blush to say, was this time a Christian prince."

"Holy Virgin!" exclaimed Iskander. "Who can this villain be?"

"The villain, Lord Iskander, is your friend; and your pupil, dear father."

"Nicæus of Athens!" exclaimed Hunniades.

Iskander was silent and melancholy.

Thereupon the Lady Iduna recounted to her father and Iskander, sitting between them on the margin of the fount, all that had occurred to her, since herself and Nicæus parted with Iskander; nor did she omit to relate to Hunniades all the devotion of Iskander, respecting which, like a truly brave man, he had himself been silent. The great Hunniades scarcely knew which rather to do, to lavish his affection on his beloved child, or his gratitude upon Iskander. Thus they went on conversing for some time, Iskander placing his own cloak around Iduna, and almost unconsciously winding his arm around her unresisting form.

Just as they were preparing to return to the Christian camp, a great noise was heard in the grove, and presently, in the direction whence Iduna had arrived, there came a band of men bearing torches and examining the grove in all directions in great agitation. Iskander and Hunniades stood upon their guard, but soon perceived they were Greeks. Their leader, seeing a group near the fountain, advanced to make inquiries respecting the object of his search, but when he indeed recognised the persons who formed the group, the torch fell from his grasp, and he turned away his head and hid his face in his hands.

Iduna clung to her father; Iskander stood with his eyes fixed upon the ground, but Hunniades, stern and terrible, disembarrassing himself of the grasp of his daughter, advanced and laid his hand upon the stranger.

"Young man," said the noble father, "were it contrition instead of shame that inspired this attitude, it might be better. I have often warned you of the fatal consequences of a reckless indulgence of the passions. More than once I have predicted to you, that however great might be your confidence in your ingenuity and your resources, the hour would arrive when such a career would place you in a position as despicable as it was shameful. That hour has arrived, and that position is now filled by the Prince of Athens. You stand before the three individuals in this world whom you have most injured, and whom you were most bound to love and to protect. Here is a friend, who hazarded his prosperity and his existence for your life and your happiness. And you have made him a mere pander to your lusts, and then deserted him in his greatest necessities. This maiden was the companion of your youth, and entitled to your kindest offices. You have treated her infinitely worse than her Turkish captor. And for myself, sir, your father was my dearest friend. I endeavoured to repay his friendship by supplying his place to his orphan child. How I discharged my duty, it becomes not me to say: how you have discharged yours, this lady here, my daughter, your late prisoner, sir, can best prove."

"Oh! spare me, spare me, sir," said the Prince of Athens, turning and falling upon his knee. "I am most wretched. Every word cuts to my very core. Just Providence has baffled all my arts, and I am grateful. Whether this lady can, indeed, forgive me, I hardly dare to think, or even hope. And yet forgiveness is a heavenly boon. Perhaps the memory of old days may melt her. As for yourself, sir—but I'll not speak, I cannot. Noble Iskander, if I mistake not, you may whisper words in that fair ear, less grating than my own. May you be happy! I will not profane your prospects with my vows. And yet I'll say farewell!"

The Prince of Athens turned away with an air of complete wretchedness, and slowly withdrew. Iskander followed him.

"Nicæus," said Iskander; but the prince entered the grove, and did not turn round.

"Dear Nicæus," said Iskander. The prince hesitated.

"Let us not part thus," said Iskander. "Iduna is most unhappy. She bade me tell you she had forgotten all."

"God bless her, and God bless you, too!" replied Nicæus. "I pray you let me go."

"Nay! dear Nicæus, are we not friends?"

"The best and truest, Iskander. I will to the camp, and meet you in your tent ere morning break. At present, I would be alone."

"Dear Nicæus, one word. You have said upon one point, what I could well wish unsaid, and dared to prophesy what may never happen. I am not made for such supreme felicity. Epirus is my mistress, my Nicæus. As there is a living God, my friend, most solemnly I vow, I have had no thoughts in this affair, but for your honour."

"I know it, my dear friend, I know it," replied Nicæus. "I keenly feel your admirable worth. Say no more, say no more! She is a fit wife for a hero, and you are one!"

CHAPTER 20

After the battle of the bridge, Iskander had hurried to Croia without delay. In his progress, he had made many fruitless inquiries after Iduna and Nicæus, but he consoled himself for the unsatisfactory answers he received by the opinion that they had taken a different course, and the conviction that all must now be safe. The messenger from Croia that informed Hunniades of the escape of his daughter, also solicited his aid in favour of Epirus against the impending invasion of the Turks, and stimulated by personal gratitude as well as by public duty, Hunniades answered the solicitation in person at the head of twenty thousand lances.

Hunniades and Iskander had mutually flattered themselves, when apart, that each would be able to quell the anxiety of the other on the subject of Iduna. The leader of Epirus flattered himself that his late companions had proceeded at once to Transylvania, and the Vaivode himself had indulged in the delightful hope that the first person he should embrace at Croia would be his long-lost child. When, therefore, they met, and were mutually incapable of imparting any information on the subject to each other, they were filled with astonishment and disquietude. Events, however, gave them little opportunity to indulge in anxiety or grief. On the day that Hunniades and his lances arrived at Croia, the invading army of the Turks under the Prince Mahomed crossed the mountains, and soon after pitched their camp on the fertile plain of Kallista.

As Iskander, by the aid of Hunniades and the neighbouring princes, and the patriotic exertions of his countrymen, was at this moment at the head of a force which the Turkish prince could not have anticipated, he resolved to march at once to meet the Ottomans, and decide the fate of Greece by a pitched battle.

The night before the arrival of Iduna at the famous fountain, the Christian army had taken up its position within a few miles of the Turks. The turbaned warriors wished to delay the engagement until the new moon, the eve of which was at hand. And it happened on that said eve that Iskander calling to mind his contract with the Turkish prince made in the gardens of the Seraglio at Adrianople, and believing from the superstitious character of Mahomed that he would not fail to be at the appointed spot, resolved, as we have seen, to repair to the fountain of Kallista.

And now from that fountain the hero retired, bearing with him a prize scarcely less precious than the freedom of his country, for which he was to combat on the morrow's morn.

Ere the dawn had broken, the Christian power was in motion. Iskander commanded the centre, Hunniades the right wing. The left was entrusted at his urgent request to the Prince of Athens. A mist that hung about the plain allowed Nicæus to charge the right wing of the Turks almost unperceived. He charged with irresistible fury, and soon disordered the ranks of the Moslemin. Mahomed with the reserve hastened to their aid. A mighty multitude of Janissaries, shouting the name of Allah and his Prophet, penetrated the Christian centre. Hunniades endeavoured to attack them on their flank, but was himself charged by the Turkish cavalry. The battle was now general, and raged with terrible fury. Iskander had secreted in his centre, a new and powerful battery of cannon, presented to him by the Pope, and which had just arrived from Venice. This battery played upon the Janissaries with great destruction. He himself mowed them down with his irresistible scimitar. Infinite was the slaughter! awful the uproar! But of all the Christian knights this day, no one performed such mighty feats of arms as the Prince of Athens. With a reckless desperation he dashed about the field, and everything seemed to yield to his inspired impulse. His example animated his men with such a degree of enthusiasm, that the division to which he was opposed, although encouraged by the presence of Mahomed himself, could no longer withstand the desperate courage of the Christians, and fled in all directions. Then, rushing to the aid of Iskander, Nicæus, at the head of a body of picked men, dashed upon the rear of the Janissaries, and nearly surrounded them. Hunniades instantly made a fresh charge upon the left wing of the Turks. A panic fell upon the Moslemin, who were little prepared for such a demonstration of strength on the part of their adversaries. In a few minutes, their order seemed generally broken, and their leaders in vain endeavoured to rally them. Waving his bloody scimitar, and bounding on his black charger, Iskander called upon his men to secure the triumph of the Cross and the freedom of Epirus. Pursuit was now general.

CHAPTER 21

The Turks were massacred by thousands. Mahomed, when he found that all was lost, fled to the mountains, with a train of guards and eunuchs, and left the care of his dispersed host to his Pachas. The hills were covered with the fugitives and their pursuers. Some fled also to the seashore, where the Turkish fleet was at anchor. The plain was strewn with corpses and arms, and tents and standards. The sun was now high in the heavens. The mist had cleared away; but occasional clouds of smoke still sailed about.

A solitary Christian knight entered a winding pass in the green hills, apart from the scene of strife. The slow and trembling step of his wearied steed would have ill qualified him to join in the triumphant pursuit, even had he himself been physically enabled; but the Christian knight was covered with gore, unhappily not alone that of his enemies. He was, indeed, streaming, with desperate wounds, and scarcely could his fainting form retain its tottering seat.

The winding pass, which for some singular reason he now pursued in solitude, instead of returning to the busy camp for aid and assistance, conducted the knight to a small green valley, covered with sweet herbs, and entirely surrounded by hanging woods. In the centre rose the ruins of a Doric fane: three or four columns, grey and majestic. All was still and silent, save that in the clear blue sky an eagle flew, high in the air, but whirling round the temple.

The knight reached the ruins of the Doric fane, and with difficulty dismounting from his charger, fell upon the soft and flowery turf, and for some moments was motionless. His horse stole a few yards away, and though scarcely less injured than its rider, instantly commenced cropping the inviting pasture.

At length the Christian knight slowly raised his head, and leaning on his arm, sighed deeply. His face was very pale; but as he looked up, and perceived the eagle in the heaven, a smile played upon his pallid cheek, and his beautiful eye gleamed with a sudden flash of light.

"Glorious bird!" murmured the Christian warrior, "once I deemed that my career might resemble thine! 'Tis over now and Greece, for which I would have done so much, will soon forget my immemorial name. I have stolen here to die in silence and in beauty. This blue air, and these green woods, and these lone columns, which oft to me have been a consolation, breathing of the poetic past, and of the days wherein I fain had lived, I have escaped from the fell field of carnage to die among them. Farewell my country! Farewell to one more beautiful than Greece, farewell, Iduna!"

These were the last words of Nicæus, Prince of Athens.

CHAPTER 22

While the unhappy lover of the daughter of Hunniades breathed his last words to the solitary elements, his more fortunate friend received, in the centre of his scene of triumph, the glorious congratulations of his emancipated country. The discomfiture of the Turks was complete, and this overthrow, coupled with their recent defeat in Bulgaria, secured Christendom from their assaults during the remainder of the reign of Amurath the Second. Surrounded by his princely allies, and the chieftains of Epirus, the victorious standards of Christendom, and the triumphant trophies of the Moslemin, Iskander received from the great Hunniades the hand of his beautiful daughter. "Thanks to these brave warriors," said the hero, "I can now offer to your daughter a safe, an honourable, and a Christian home."

"It is to thee, great sir, that Epirus owes its security," said an ancient chieftain, addressing Iskander, "its national existence, and its holy religion. All that we have to do now is to preserve them; nor indeed do I see that we can more effectually obtain these great objects than by entreating thee to mount the redeemed throne of thy ancestors. Therefore I say GOD SAVE ISKANDER, KING OF EPIRUS!"

And all the people shouted and said, "GOD SAVE THE KING! GOD SAVE ISKANDER, KING OF EPIRUS!"